Praise for

Lauren in the Limelight

"This is the book I wish I could have read as a young ballet student."

—**MEGAN FAIRCHILD**, principal dancer with New York City Ballet and author of *The Ballerina Mindset*

"I so wish that *Lauren in the Limelight* had been in my local library when I was a tween-ager . . . I would have loved loved loved to imagine myself Lauren then and I know that tweens—ballet fans or not—are going to love it now."

—**NANCY PEARL**, author of the Book Lust series and *George & Lizzie: A Novel*

"*Lauren in the Limelight* promotes empathy and understanding and deals with the crucial moments in life when we gain maturity, break from our parents' version of us, and become ourselves."

—**PETER BOAL**, Artistic Director of Pacific Northwest Ballet and author of *Illusions of Camelot*

"*Lauren in the Limelight* centers around three young adolescents captivated by ballet's mysterious, magical lure, but this book is about so much more than dance. The characters' relationship and fascination with ballet is a prism through which we—and they—begin to discover and understand the complexities of self-identity, autonomy, and morality and that adults have just as many internal conflicts as kids."

—**GAVIN LARSEN,** author of *Being a Ballerina* and former principal with Oregon Ballet Theatre

"We love stories about dancers written by dancers! *Lauren in the Limelight* is a novel perfect for young dancers starting their journey into pointe work."

—**KATHRYN MORGAN,** former soloist with New York City Ballet

"It has everything. Drama. Competition. Passion. If you love ballet, you will love Miriam Landis's book."

—**MARY HELEN BOWERS,** Founder and CEO of Ballet Beautiful

GIRL IN MOTION

Also by Miriam Landis

Lauren in the Limelight

Girl on Pointe
(previously published as *Breaking Pointe*)

GIRL IN MOTION

a novel

MIRIAM LANDIS

Rhododendron Press
Seattle

Girl in Motion

Previously published by CreateSpace in 2010
First Rhododendron Press printing, October 2023

For information about this title or to order other books and/or electronic media, contact the publisher:

Rhododendron
Press

www.rhododendronpress.com

ISBNs:
979-8-9883078-3-9 (softcover)
979-8-9883078-4-6 (eBook)

Printed in the United States of America

Cover and Interior design: 1106 Design

Cover image of Sarah-Gabrielle Ryan copyright © Dan Lao

Typeset in Adobe Garamond Pro

For Daniel

Author's Note

I remember exactly where I sat in the winter of 2003 when I wrote *Girl in Motion's* first words. The Mirrielees apartments at Stanford University housed approximately 340 students, but I was the only resident who had been a professional ballerina. As a twenty-four-year-old junior, I was older than most undergraduates. There were two other retired dancers in the class of 2004, and all of us had been well into our twenties on our first days on campus. A few days earlier, weeks before taking the MCAT, I'd left the premed track and switched my major from Human Biology to English Literature.

There I was, wondering how I'd gone so far down another career path and why, once again, I was changing directions. I began to write, hoping to figure myself out.

Later, a few years into my editorial career at a major New York publishing house, I realized that an endless number of books originate from an author's sentiment that "no one understands what I've been through." And for good reason—in the twenty years between my writing days at the Mirrielees apartments and this copy of *Girl in Motion* landing in your hands, I reached a deeper understanding of how unique and mystifying a dancer's journey is.

I grew up reading every ballet book and watching every ballet film I could get my hands on. If ballet was to be my life—and I knew it was from a very young age—the immersion was about so much more than what I learned in the studio. The book and movie options were slim. There's not much in the media about ballet beyond outstanding nonfiction. You can count on one hand the number of novels written for and about dancers during the most critical training years.

At the Mirrielees dorm desk and during the quarter I spent studying abroad in Paris, I wrote and wrote for my younger self, the dancer who was so in love with ballet that she gave up all the typical teenage experiences. From the age of twelve, when I went on pointe, until the age of twenty-one, I had thought I knew what I was doing. I had been so sure.

Writing was how I crawled through the years of wishing I'd done it all differently. Eventually, I grew up enough to understand who I was beyond my all-encompassing dancer identity. By then, I'd had a stellar literary agent and collected rejections from the biggest publishing houses. I heard that ballet was too niche and marketing dance stories was problematic, but the real issue was that I was writing but hadn't learned the craft of fiction. If I wanted to be a writer, I had to train the same way I'd learned how to be a dancer: a little bit every day, for decades.

I was a corporate publishing professional on the Amazon Books team—as far from my ballet career as could be—when Amazon launched its first self-publishing platform, CreateSpace. My husband convinced me to self-publish *Girl in Motion* and the sequel, then titled *Breaking Pointe* (now *Girl on Pointe* because the first title turned into a reality TV show). We released the books a decade after I'd written them and we were pleasantly shocked that over 10,000 copies sold.

Content with what I'd done, I spent the next decade building a family and finding my way back to the studio as a ballet teacher. I kept writing as a blogger for my local indie bookstore and working privately on the craft of fiction. The creative process nurtured the artist within me who couldn't stop dancing.

Fast forward to the pandemic. I wrote *Lauren in the Limelight* when COVID-19 kept most of the world home. It was a story specific to tweens, a group I'd missed with my first two books. The ballet world changed rapidly during that time, and as a Pacific Northwest Ballet School faculty member, I watched it up close, in real time. We were at the forefront, struggling to do better and prioritize inclusivity and mental health in a way I could have only dreamed about as a ballet student and professional.

Now in my forties, I'm closer to answering, "Why did I do all that?" I suspect many people find answers mid-life. After two years of querying agents and publishers with *Lauren in the Limelight* and hearing again that ballet was too niche, I published it myself. I founded Rhododendron Press with the knowledge I'd gained from my years in the publishing and ballet industries combined.

In 2023, I completed *Lauren in the Limelight*. At the same time, I revisited the books I'd written in my twenties, seeing their characters anew through my eyes as a mother, an instructor, and a person who cares deeply for the next generation. I continue sharing this art form I love through my studio teaching and solitary writing. I want others to know classical ballet and understand its discipline and immense rewards—it's my way of contributing to the future of ballet and those who will inhabit it. My books were written for the people who bring this art form to life. I want them to find fiction on the shelves to accompany their journeys in the dance world. Whether you're a dancer, a dance lover, or a person who has a dream and follows it, I invite you to find a bit of yourself in my characters' challenges, wonders, and triumphs.

As ever,

Miriam Landis
September 1, 2023

CHAPTER 1

I was a dancer from the beginning.

At two, I walked across our kitchen floor on my tiptoes. At ten, I read every ballet book I could get my hands on, and my ballet teacher became the most important person in my life outside my family. At thirteen, I spent every day after school at ballet class, images of princesses, swans, and tutus floating through my mind. At sixteen, I knew I wanted to be a professional.

It was a few days after my birthday. When I woke up and looked outside, fresh snow covered the roads and piled up against my bedroom window. My entire life, I'd lived in Rock Island, Illinois, and my small town looked sleepier than ever. Sure, I wished I had a boyfriend like the popular girls at my high school, but I'd just passed my driving test and had the lead in the spring recital. My parents were still married and loved me. What did I have to complain about?

The problem was that I needed more. My ambitions were wildly different from those of my friends.

Our tabby cat, Oliver, opened my door with his nose and meowed. He marched in with his tail in the air. "Come here, you," I said, but he only let me scratch his ears for a second before he turned in a circle and left. My mom said he was her cat, and he was. No matter how hard I tried to win him over he followed her everywhere.

I put on my robe and followed the smell of pancakes and syrup. The framed pictures in the hallway captured my childhood. There I was, at eight, standing by the family station wagon on a road trip to Wisconsin Dells, and at twelve, in a pink tutu with a mouth full of braces. My favorite was the photo of Mom, Dad, and me at my aunt's wedding in Indianapolis. Dad's glasses were crooked, and Mom's eyes were red from all her tears, but she had three-year-old me balanced on one hip. I was wearing the frilliest dress in the world and had chocolate cake smeared across my face.

Today, I could tell Dad was fired up from the sound of dishes clattering, and I could hear him lecturing Mom on safe driving in bad weather. He kept saying he didn't understand why we had to drive to Chicago on a Saturday in the middle of winter.

"You'll have time to grade papers while we're gone," Mom said. Dad was an English professor at the nearby university.

"Margaret says Anna is the most talented student she's ever had, and she's owned that ballet school since I was a kid," Mom said, sipping her coffee so loudly that I could hear her in the hall. "Look at our daughter, Frank. God knows she didn't get it from us, but she has that bone structure and face. Her feet and flexibility are ideal. Margaret insists that if we're serious about this, we should send Anna to a school attached to a famous company. The School of Ballet New York—sorry, everyone calls it SBNY—is the most prestigious. Ballet New York is one of the top companies in the world, and they only accept dancers from the school."

Dad's tone made it clear he still wasn't taking her seriously. "Thousands of kids audition for this summer program," he said. "I read the flyer. You and I have two left feet. How could Anna be professional material? They only pick two hundred from the audition tour, and out of that group, they only ask a handful to stay for the school year. We have two years left before she goes to college, and there's no way we're sending her to boarding school with that expense on the horizon."

"I'm not getting a degree, so you don't need to worry about tuition," I said, walking into the kitchen. "I have to get into a company by the time I'm eighteen. That's how it works. Professional dancers don't go to college."

Dad started shouting, and Mom put her face in her hands.

That afternoon at one o'clock, Mom and I stood in the waiting room of the ballet school in downtown Chicago. Suddenly, she looked so small-town, with her floral dress and bag of knitting in hand, just an ordinary woman who worked as a receptionist in an orthodontist's office. Her hair was cut short around her ears. She never bothered with makeup.

"I wonder what would have happened if I kept dancing in high school," she said. "Maybe I'd have done an audition like this." She kept shifting from one foot to the other, and her eyes darted around the room. Once we'd paid the audition fee and pinned my number to my black leotard, she kissed me goodbye and wished me luck. There were already forty kids in the line for my age group, all girls except for six boys.

The two women running the audition directed us to stand at the barre in numerical order. One wore a suit and heels. She had a stern face and short gray hair. The other was younger and prettier, with the most defined and muscular body I'd ever seen. She'd twisted her long hair in a top knot and wore a unitard and floral chiffon skirt. Everything about them conveyed seriousness and purpose.

We stood there silently as they went from one of us to the next, asking us to point our feet. The younger woman lifted our legs to each side to see how high they could go, and the other took notes. Every kid in the room looked terrified.

After they'd gone through everyone, the older and more intimidating woman walked to the front of the room and said, "Thank you all for coming. My name is Madame Sivenko, and I'm the school principal. This is Vivienne Lalane, and she'll teach your audition class."

Madame Sivenko sat down behind a table at the front of the room. There were index cards carefully laid out in front of her, presumably one for each of us. She made notes on the cards throughout the audition.

The blonde girl beside me angled her head toward Madame Sivenko and whispered, "Did you know she was a famous ballerina with the Ballet Russe back in the day? And the teacher is a former principal with Ballet New York.

I inched away from the girl, worried they'd think I was the one talking.

Vivienne Lalane sparkled with energy and confidence. She circled the room as we executed each combination, looking for inherent attributes: highly arched feet, long legs, natural hip turnout, and flexibility. My teacher Margaret had reassured me I looked the part. How my ballet friends at home treated me constantly reinforced that I had what it took. Everyone knew I was the best there.

But for the first time, I wasn't sure I had the upper hand, even though I held my chin up and went first across the floor. I sized up the other dancers and could see I was still at the top, but two others had higher extensions and better turns than me. I felt OK about how I danced, but Madame Sivenko looked at the other two more than anyone else.

"I can't believe you're going to miss prom because of your ballet recital," Rachel said, twisting her blonde ponytail. We'd come to my house after school to try and finish a social studies project, but all we'd done was gossip on my bed for an hour.

She lived six houses away and had never understood my ballet obsession, but she accepted it. While I danced six days a week, she played tennis, joined the school paper and student government, and chased boys. We'd hung out at each other's houses and talked on the phone every night for as long as I could remember.

"Who would I go with?" I asked. She knew I'd never had a real boyfriend. Most people at our high school only knew me as a serious student who wore her hair in a bun.

She stood and studied her tall, curvy, athletic body in my full-length mirror. "It's not fair you're so petite and shaped like a stick," she said.

"I've been running to the mailbox every day for six weeks," I said, flopping backward on my bed and flexing my feet. "When is that letter going to come?"

"We can still find you a date," Rachel said. "You're pretty *and* nice. Who wouldn't want to go with you?"

I didn't tell her I didn't care. All I could think about was getting in.

As I did every day, the next afternoon, I went straight to the mailbox when I came home from school. There was a slim white envelope with SBNY on the return address. It looked too thin to be an acceptance letter.

My hands shook as I carried the mail inside.

I handed the letter to Mom and asked her to open it. The grandfather clock in the hallway chimed the hour. While she tore the envelope, I sank into a living room chair and put my hands over my eyes.

She startled me with her shout of enthusiasm. My head snapped up. There was a hint of regret when she said, "It looks like you're going to New York."

My path was more apparent than ever. Mom never asked if I wanted to go because she already knew.

CHAPTER 2

Margaret said that I'd see that at SBNY, everyone was the top student from their hometown. She wished me luck and told me she was proud.

At the airport, Mom cried and Dad hugged me and said, "Prepare to be ordinary. Someone like me prefers to be a big fish in a small pond. That's why I took tenure in Rock Island and raised my family here. But being a small fish in a big pond is OK when you're young. You'll see if you like it, and you can always come home."

I didn't tear up until the airplane was on the runway. An nice lady offered me a tissue.

Flying, dragging my duffel bags from baggage claim to the curb, and getting a taxi alone were significant firsts. I felt proud of myself when the cab crossed the Queensboro Bridge into Manhattan. When I saw the skyscrapers for the first time, my stomach turned over. I'd read about New York and seen it in movies and on television since I was little, but I wasn't ready for the nervousness and anticipation of being there in person. This milestone was more than a five-week summer program to me; it was an audition. They only asked a handful of students back for the school year. I was determined to be one of them.

My brain hummed as we drove through the West Side of Manhattan. The cabbie was friendly and talkative, but I couldn't understand his broken English. He pointed toward Central Park, and I craned my neck to glimpse the trees through the side streets.

When I climbed out of the cab, the air was humid and smelled of car exhaust. The Roizman building, located in a massive complex at Lincoln Center, stood there like something out of a legend.

I took it all in. Me. At the center of the dance world.

I took the elevators to the dorm with a group of moms and daughters, which made me wish my parents could have dropped me off. Two moms were excited when they realized they'd both driven from Ohio. Their daughters looked nervous until a pale, waifish redhead with an upturned nose and freckles said this was her third summer and they shouldn't worry. One of the Ohio moms added, "These kids dance five days a week and have three classes daily: technique, pointe, variations, *pas de deux*, jazz, modern, and character dance. They won't have time to be homesick."

The inside of the building was new, with thick blue carpeting and pictures of famous dancers on the walls.

I waited in line to check in and get my room key. The resident assistant said I was on a girls-only floor, in a suite with three double rooms and a communal bathroom. The laundry room was near the elevator.

I opened the door to my suite for a girl who had followed me down the hall. "Are you Anna?" she asked in a charming Southern accent.

"That's me," I said, smiling back at her.

She was tall and pretty with dimples. "I'm your new roommate, Kristen."

Our room was tiny, with just enough space to walk around the bunk bed. Another girl in the suite said our rooms were used as singles during the school year.

Kristen and I talked nonstop for the next two hours while we unpacked. She showed me a picture of her boyfriend. He was the best-looking guy I'd seen, much cuter than the jock Rachel went to prom with.

I'd never met anyone from North Carolina before, and she'd never met anyone from Illinois. We couldn't believe how much we had in common. She shared my love for the Beatles, chocolate mousse cake, striped leg warmers, jeweled hair clips, and tacos.

"I signed up for the weekend trips to the Met Museum and the Statue of Liberty," she said as we took the elevator to the cafeteria. "Did you?"

It was clear we were going to spend every minute together.

The redheaded girl I'd rode the elevator with earlier walked out of the cafeteria as we walked in. She'd put a lot of makeup on and looked older than she had that afternoon. "You two make a funny pair," she said, breezing past us while we exchanged a confused look.

"That has to be Hilary Marshall," Kristen whispered. "A girl I know who came here last year warned me about her. She said Hilary's mean and told everyone that all the big ballet schools offered her scholarships every year since she was twelve."

"Is it true?" I asked.

Kristen glanced around to check that no one heard us. "I don't know."

We collected our trays and joined the crowd, wandering from food station to food station, and I realized what Hilary meant about us being a funny pair. I was one of the shortest, and Kristen was one of the tallest kids there.

Hilary's comment planted a seed of worry. How big of a problem was it that I didn't look exactly like everyone else?

After we crawled into bed and turned off the reading lamp that night, Kristen leaned over the top bunk and said, "I miss my boyfriend. Do you know he told me I was beautiful, even after I got my wisdom teeth out? I looked like a chipmunk. Do you have a boyfriend at home?"

"No," I confessed. "Not a real one." What I didn't say was that I couldn't imagine a cute boy liking me. The boys my age back home could be so immature.

She said, "We grew up together because our moms were friends in college. I don't remember not knowing him."

The lights from Lincoln Center shined through our window, their glow casting shadows across the room.

The atmosphere was full of tension and excitement when I stepped off the elevators on the first day of ballet class. Kristen and I stood in the lobby momentarily to take it in. Girls were rushing off to class with their hair in tight buns. A few mothers stood by the front desk, watching their kids go beyond the sign that said, "No Parents Beyond this Point," and complaining to each other about pointe shoe prices.

I leaned over to Kristen and whispered, "Is it just me, or does this place feel like the mothership of childhood hopes and dreams?"

She took my arm and pulled me past the parents' area. We'd checked the dorm's bulletin board and knew our first class was with Simon Saunders in Studio C. We'd both placed in the second-to-highest level. I was a little disappointed but glad we were together.

There were dancers spread out all over the hallway floors, stretching and putting on pointe shoes.

"Look," Kristen said, pointing at a picture of a striking male ballet dancer in white tights, a white tunic, and white ballet slippers. The man posed with his arm extended forward as if gesturing to a partner. He was all defined muscle, broad chest, and celebrity-level beauty.

"That's Victor Caldwell," said a voice behind us. It was the redhead named Hilary again. When Kristen and I gave her a blank look, she continued, "You know—the king of the empire—the artistic director of Ballet New York. He was a famous principal dancer here. The board appointed him the artistic director ten years ago, right before Nicholas Roizman died."

I'd read a little about Victor Caldwell and Nicholas Roizman in the SNBY brochure and an old ballet book Margaret kept in her waiting room.

"He's so good-looking," Kristen said.

Hilary tilted her head and cracked her neck before saying, "Anyone who followed a legend like Nicholas Roizman was bound to be controversial. Ballet New York is the best company in the world, and SBNY isn't just any ballet school; it's *the* ballet school. Roizman said it all starts with the students.

I said, "With us."

Hilary picked up her bag and walked toward Studio A. "You got it," she said over her shoulder.

Kristen stared after her. "Well, isn't she special?" We exchanged a look. Hilary was a know-it-all.

I asked, "Do you know if Victor Caldwell will be here this summer?"

"The company is in upstate New York for their summer residency," she said as we headed toward class. "I doubt it."

We were half an hour early, but inside Studio C, a few other girls had already arrived. Kristen and I pulled one of the portable barres away from the wall. We lined it up on the crack between mirrors and took spots on either side.

"How's your mirror?" Kristen asked.

I turned sideways and checked myself out. "It's pretty good. How's yours?"

"This one isn't doing me any favors," she said, frowning.

Simon Saunders came into the room. Everyone was nervous because he was one of the most famous ballet teachers ever. He had white hair and a kind, gentle face. In person, he was more ordinary-looking than in the pictures I'd seen. For a man who coached the most famous dancers in the world, I'd expected to see magic sparks shoot from his head.

As we stood in first position to start our *pliés*, I wondered how he could tell us apart in our black leotards, pink tights, and tight buns. I wanted to fit in so much. Even more, I wanted to stand out.

I was scared. We all were. And yet, every pair of eyes in the room shined with excitement.

During the first week, I learned how many dance legends co-existed on the Upper West Side. Within two days, I saw a guest star from the Royal Danish Ballet taking the men's class at SBNY, a ballet master from Ballet New York walking in as I walked out of the New York Library for the Performing Arts, and the current leading BNY ballerina buying skin cream at Rite Aid. I stood behind her and studied the long line of her neck and how she'd tied a scarf around her waist like a skirt. There was a bandage around her ankle like she'd sprained it, which explained why she was still in the city.

On Saturday, after the first week of classes, Kristen and I joined the school trip to the Metropolitan Museum of Art. As we studied the Degas paintings, she asked, "Is BNY your dream company?"

"Isn't it for everyone?" I asked, embarrassed by how eager I sounded. When she didn't respond, I added, "What about you?"

She hesitated. "To be honest," she said, "I'm not sure I want to dance professionally. I'm only sixteen. Is it stupid to say I'm more interested in getting married? I'm not sure the two go together."

I let that sink in. It was the first moment of friction between us. What did she think this was, summer camp? Did she realize she'd taken a top spot away from someone who would have deeply appreciated the chance to attend SBNY and recognized the opportunity for what it was? Part of me was relieved that she wasn't in it to win.

"I can't even think about getting married," I said, surprised that her thoughts differed from mine.

We stayed up late that night talking. She wanted to continue our conversation from the museum and went on about what it would be like if she married her boyfriend. I listened while she described how they'd have two kids, spend their weekends barbecuing with friends, and go on exciting trips while the grandparents babysat. Maybe they'd fix up a house on his salary.

She reminded me of my friend Rachel back home, bringing a familiar sadness that someone I liked was heading down a different path.

As the second week began, it became even clearer from the sloppy way she did her hair and how she daydreamed in class that Kristen genuinely had no long-term interest in New York or a serious ballet career. She admitted that she only came to SBNY because her parents and ballet teachers convinced her she couldn't throw away the opportunity.

By week three, as I grew more anxious about receiving an invitation for fall, Kristen's talk about her boyfriend made me feel like screaming. Didn't she realize how silly she sounded?

Sometimes, she looked at me like I was the crazy one. Maybe I was. Kristen could already see life beyond the studio and stage. But I couldn't. I just couldn't.

At the beginning of the fourth week, I overheard Madame Sivenko talking to a nervous mother in the hallway. "They're here for such a short time in the summer," Madame Sivenko said curtly, "I'm sorry to say we can't invest in everyone."

"What do you mean by that?" the woman asked.

"We can only do so much for our summer students. It's our year-round program that produces professionals."

"I'm counting on my daughter being here in the fall," the mother said. "I have questions. What do your students do about academics?"

Madame Sivenko checked her expensive-looking watch. "Our boarding students generally attend Young Artist's High—YAH—on West 60th Street," she said. "The school accommodates dancers, actors, and musicians with professional schedules. A few do correspondence, which means they earn their GED by completing their coursework by mail.

The students must focus primarily on their SBNY classes. For a dancer to succeed, ballet must be the top priority."

The mom had done her homework. "Ballet is everything to us. My daughter is very talented, as I'm sure you've noticed, and—"

I wondered who the woman's daughter was and felt embarrassed for that girl.

"Excuse me," Madame Sivenko said, cutting her off. "I need to go."

The standards were so high. It was so tough to get in.

As Madame Sivenko hurried down the hall, I wondered how often she had that conversation with other parents.

Whatever it took to succeed, I needed to figure it out fast. If I didn't, I'd be heading home in a week. For good.

On the last Saturday of the program, Kristen and I skipped the cafeteria and went out for dinner at a Chinese restaurant. When we returned to the dorms, there was a group gossiping at the front desk.

"What's going on?" I asked the Brazilian girl who lived in the suite across the hall from ours.

"They just sent that girl from Texas home," she said. "She got caught stealing money from her roommate. Why would anyone blow their chances here by doing something so stupid, especially on the last weekend?"

"Why do you smell like that?" Kristen asked the Brazilian girl, and that's when I realized she smelled like the beer my dad sometimes drank.

"They've got stuff in suite 101," the Brazilian girl said. "But you are probably too goody-goody for it. Don't tell anyone or those kids will kill me."

"Aren't people worried about blowing a year-round invitation?" I asked, proving she was right about me being a goody-goody.

"They already asked four people back. I guess everyone else figures that's it. The decision has been made. The school gets to choose us, not the other way around. What's wrong with blowing off a little steam if they don't want us?"

This was all news to me. Four people? Who? I thought I had a few more days before I'd know if I'd been passed over.

"Are you OK?" Kristen asked me.

I managed to say, "Who got asked back?"

The Brazilian girl mentioned two boys, one girl I didn't know, and Hilary Marshall, the redheaded know-it-all. Of course.

I was so discouraged that I almost didn't go to class on Monday, and if Kristen hadn't been there to drag me out of bed, I probably would have stayed there the entire week. So many fears and worries overtook me, and I couldn't think straight. How could I go back to life and my little ballet school in Rock Island and pretend this summer and this huge dream I'd had never even happened?

Everything was a blur. I sleepwalked through my classes.

We'd gone to our dorm suite on Thursday after lunch for a quick break before variation class. I was changing leotards when Kristen called from the outer room, "Anna, your dad is calling."

"I'll be there in a second," I hollered, studying myself in the dresser mirror. I reapplied hairspray to my bun. It was a strange time of day for him to call.

A moment later, Kristen appeared in the doorway and asked, "Are you going outside to call him back? I can go ahead to class if you want privacy."

"I'll take it here this time," I said. "You can go, thanks."

Why was Dad calling in the middle of the day? He was usually busy at work, and I was two hours ahead in New York.

I walked into the hall and put the phone to my ear. Dad said hello and told me how Oliver carried a dead rat through the house that morning.

I interrupted him with, "Is everything okay?"

My mind tried out different reasons for a call in the middle of the afternoon. Maybe my aunt drove up to visit and wanted to say hello. Maybe Mom was sick. Maybe my flight home had been canceled.

"We just got a call from Madame Sivenko," Dad said.

My heart stopped.

Mom came on the line. "Dad was home for lunch today, and it was the strangest thing: the phone rang, and we stared at it—"

"You got a call from *Madame Sivenko?*"

She laughed with pleasure. Dad waited, drawing out the suspense.

"You've been invited back," he said.

I couldn't help it. I screamed.

It didn't seem real.

"We know how desperately you wanted this," Mom said.

I bit my nails and asked, "Does this mean I can move here for junior year?"

"Would it stop you if we said no?" Mom asked.

Dad said, "It's going to be a huge stretch financially, but I don't see how to talk you out of it—"

"You can't." Saying the words felt exhilarating. Was this happening? Was I old enough to move to New York on my own?

Dad said, "There's only one good job in ballet. I'm talking about the prima ballerina of Ballet New York. Everyone else is just trying to claw their way up. Who is it again? Stacy Hannah, right?"

He knew I studied *Dance Magazine* like it was the Bible. "It's Diana Rampling now," I corrected, marveling that

I'd stood right behind her in Rite Aid a few weeks earlier. "Stacy Hannah retired."

"I always think of Stacy Hannah and William Mason together," Mom said. "They were the big stars of BNY when I was a kid."

"Diana Rampling. That's the one I meant," Dad said in an amused tone. "Well, I guess you'll be the next Diana Rampling."

Once-in-a-lifetime opportunities didn't happen to anyone I knew, most of all to me. Fear crept in. Maybe I wasn't ready to leave home after all.

I had to be brave. I'd worked too hard for too long to turn back now. Mom and Dad waited patiently while I talked it through.

"We're happy because you're happy," Mom said.

Dad added, "Not because we want you to be a professional dancer."

They didn't understand. I had so much passion for ballet that I didn't know how to express it. All I could say was, "I'm going to get into Ballet New York. Wait and see."

After the summer course, I spent two weeks at home, trying to pack my life into two duffle bags. Rachel hung out at my house almost every night and helped me pack. Oliver sat in an empty dresser drawer, licking his paws and watching me accusingly.

After Rachel said goodbye and left for the last time, I stretched out on my bedroom floor and felt a rush of nostalgia for home.

"Come to the table for dinner," Mom called up the stairs. I loved my family and friends. The small things made my heart feel heavy.

While I relished the comfort of my childhood, I couldn't wait to be surrounded by people who understood me on a different level. I was eager and ready to start my new life in New York.

CHAPTER 3

I forced myself to close the autobiography I'd been reading when the plane touched down at JFK. The book was about a prima ballerina and her legendary partnership with a superstar male dancer, but the juicy parts were her drug addiction, romances, and eventual ruin. It was funny that when Dad gave me her memoir, he thought it would discourage me from pursuing a ballet career. I couldn't stop reading.

I was sweating when I dragged my duffel bags outside and climbed into a cab, but this time, I knew what I was doing. "Lincoln Center, please," I told the driver. The skyscrapers rose in front of me.

When I arrived at the Roizman building and rode the elevator up to the dorms, the front desk was crowded. After twenty minutes of waiting, a resident assistant I'd never seen before—a gorgeous dark-haired girl whose nametag said Nicole Ashbury—waved me over and looked me up and down.

She had sharp gray eyes, carefully lined in black. Later, I learned that Nicole was a native New Yorker and had been at the school since she was nine, but then, all I knew was how small town I felt compared to her.

She riffled through a stack of envelopes after I told her my name. "You're on the fifteenth floor. Here's your key."

I took the envelope. "Who's my roommate?"

She checked another list. "Do you know Hilary Marshall?"

My heart sank.

Nicole could see I was dismayed. "Most returning students picked people they knew at the end of last year," she said.

Hilary might be better than I thought. That was the weird thing about ballet. People acted differently in a competitive environment. I'd been surprised when kids who were mean at ballet acted nice outside the studio.

While I digested the Hilary news, Nicole turned back to her paperwork. She ran a hand through her long, silky hair. There was a gleaming emerald ring on her finger and a diamond-studded bracelet on her wrist.

Other students jostled around me, impatient for the line to move. I hurried to collect my bags.

The elevator took me up another two floors to find my room at the end of the hall. Everything felt different. The summer was temporary, but now, the school was supposed to be home.

My mind went back to Mom and what she'd be doing at that moment. She'd be at the front desk at the orthodontist's office where she'd worked most of my life. Her manner put all the nervous kids at ease. Dad would be in his office in the English Department, finishing his fall semester course outlines. Oliver was probably sitting in the front window, waiting for everyone to come home.

When I entered my dorm room, Hilary was standing there. Her suitcase, half empty, lay open on the floor. She looked over, and to my relief, there was a friendly expression on her face. Two twin beds occupied opposite sides of the room, each with a wood desk, dresser, and closet.

She said, "I hope you don't mind that I already took the bed farther from the door. You get the newer desk."

I tossed my duffels on the bed closest to me. "Good to see you again." I said cautiously.

She pulled her long copper hair over one shoulder and crossed her arms, leaning back against her bed. The silence stretched on and became awkward as we looked at each other. I took in her muscled legs and elegant shoulders.

"They've asked me to stay for two years in a row, and my parents kept saying I was too young," Hilary said, returning to her suitcase and taking out a pile of leotards. "I hope I don't end up in a lower level just because I turned them down before."

I started unpacking too. The sight of my alarm clock and jewelry box felt like a life raft.

"Are you going to Young Artists High?" she asked.

"Yes," I said, arranging shampoo and conditioner in my shower caddy. "You?"

She was bending over in the corner, so her voice was muffled when she said, "I'm doing correspondence. Who has time for school? I'm here for ballet."

That was when I realized she had a TV. Her own TV to keep in our room, the kind with a decent-size screen and everything. She'd hoisted it out of a box and turned to lift it onto her dresser so that it faced both our beds. There was a public one in the lounge on every floor, but a TV in the room was a huge step up.

Maybe this wouldn't be so bad. But had I made a mistake enrolling in YAH? My parents thought that at least some face time at school with teachers and kids outside of SBNY would be beneficial. But maybe Hilary was right. Perhaps I wasn't as laser-focused on my ballet training as I should be.

I turned away from her and arranged my leotards and tights in a drawer. The more I looked at my cheap and ordinary belongings, the smaller I felt. This wasn't a place for shabby clothes and plastic shower caddies. Only my pile of brand-new shiny peach pointe shoes looked expensive enough to be there.

I did my best to make the room feel like home by hanging pictures of my family and friends on the bulletin board over my bed.

"You're organized," Hilary commented as she slung a leopard-print purse over her shoulder. She said she had finished unpacking. She asked if I wanted to explore Lincoln Center with her, but I declined. After she left, my eyes ran across her makeup tray and fluffy throw pillows. I took off the lid and stole a whiff of her perfume. I wished Kristen had returned for the year and was still my roommate. She was probably on a date with her boyfriend at that very moment.

I was grateful to have the room to myself for a while. I'd never shared a room with anyone before summer. Kristen had been a good experience, but Hilary and I seemed different.

When I finished, I sat down on the window ledge. I could look straight down onto the plaza far below, and beyond the open expanse, I could see the Metropolitan Opera House and a corner of the New York State Theater. The view made me feel even more insignificant.

Hilary and I went to dinner a few hours later. The more we talked, the more I could see how much I could learn from her. But almost everything she said made me feel insecure.

"I hope the food is better than in the summer," Hilary said, charging ahead of me into the cafeteria. I stopped to gather silverware and napkins.

"You're new," a confident voice said behind me. I looked up into a pair of blue eyes. "I'm Tyler," said a boy with dimples and brown hair. He was about five foot nine, with feet too big for his body, broad shoulders, and a skinny but well-proportioned build.

I stared stupidly as he headed past me toward the food. He walked like a duck.

"You can sit with me," Tyler called over his shoulder. "But I can't stand girls who don't eat."

A rush of adrenaline came over me. "I eat," I called. Kristen and I always sat with girls during the summer. At home, when Rachel talked to the boys, I hung back. This was new.

I'd been asked if I was anorexic many times, but honestly, I didn't know the line between normal eating and what I did. The topic made me anxious. My mom constantly refilled my plate mid-meal, but I felt guilty about eating. How could I not? The message had a much weaker signal in Rock Island, but it was all around me at SBNY. Aesthetics mattered.

Any discussions about weight brought a rush of negative feelings for every girl I knew, no matter what size we were. I'd often heard, "You're lucky you're naturally thin." While people intended it as a compliment, the words made me feel guilty.

Hilary was pouring milk into two bowls of cereal. It made me sad that her dinner was Cheerios. I whispered, "Let's sit with the guy in the blue shirt, OK?"

She looked at Tyler and said, "He's cute. I bet he's a good partner, too."

I went to fix a plate with small portions of penne and broccoli. Hilary met me at the cashier's line. We had our meal cards scanned, then walked into the dining area toward Tyler's table, where he was sitting with two other boys. Hilary stepped in front of me and took the seat across from him.

I took the odd seat out as we introduced ourselves. The two other boys said they were juniors, like Hilary and me, and starting their second year away at SBNY. Tyler made eye contact and smiled. "I'm a sophomore. The baby in this group of old people."

"I'm not exactly new to SNBY," Hilary said. "I've been here a few summers in a row."

Charlie, a skinny boy with blonde curls beside Tyler, said, "That doesn't count, Red. The school year is a completely different beast. Tell her, Jesse."

A third boy snorted but said nothing. He was as good-looking as Tyler but far more intimidating, with darker hair, intense eyebrows, and a severe manner. He looked more like a football player than a ballet dancer, with a broad chest and ripped arms on full display thanks to his white tank top.

Charlie continued, "We were wondering if Simon will return from the Royal Danish to teach our first class on Monday. We have that gorgeous BNY soloist, Matthew Talroy, for the rest of the week." As he said the last sentence, Charlie knocked over his glass of soda. We laughed as he wiped up the mess.

"We're at a cramped cafeteria table here, Charlie," Jesse said. "Stop talking with your hands all the time." He had a low voice and sounded much more grown-up than the others.

I wondered how good of a dancer each of the boys was.

Tyler laughed, a warm, infectious sound. His dimples showed even more when he was amused.

Charlie smacked Jesse's shoulder. "Scoot over if I'm bothering you," Charlie said.

Jesse bit into his hamburger. After a moment, he caught me staring at him. I could only meet his gaze for a few seconds before I felt my face heat up.

We ate, watching people move through the cafeteria.

The food tasted bland. I said, "I have a question. Is Madame Sivenko mean, or just scary? It was hard to tell during the summer."

The boys stared at me as if I'd announced the sky was blue.

"We'll take that as a yes," Hilary said. "What else? I want to know all the secrets. Tell us the hot gossip."

"Madame Sivenko is scary more than mean," Tyler said after a minute. "But she could make or break your career, so you better hope she likes you."

Jesse wiped his mouth with a napkin. He stood, picked up his tray, and said, "If I were you, I wouldn't talk about the teachers too much. Nicole says the walls have ears."

Charlie swung his arms out to indicate that hidden microphones were everywhere.

"That can't be true," I said. Tyler patted my hand reassuringly. My crush on him grew with every minute. Maybe I'd get to dance with him in partnering class.

Hilary said, "It wouldn't surprise me."

Ballet classes began two days later. Young Artist's High didn't start until the following week, so I had more time to get ready on the first day and spent an hour doing and redoing my hair, trying to look as perfect as possible. I sprayed it wet, pulled it into a tight ponytail, twisted it into a figure eight, clipped it to my head, and jammed in bobby pin after bobby pin until my scalp hurt. When it looked perfect from all angles, I sprayed everything down with hairspray.

Next came mascara, sand-colored lipstick, and powder. I wore my new black leotard with velvet straps, pink tights, grey knit legwarmer pants, purple ballet sweater, and black bedroom slippers.

Hilary was ready in half the time and left to go downstairs and warm up long before me. Before I left our room, I stood in front of the mirror, willing myself to be good. After all my efforts, I was frustrated that I still didn't look right. I didn't know why.

Our class assignments were posted outside the studios in the waiting area on the fifth floor. There were two levels in the girls' upper division and thirty students in each class. I was disappointed to see my name in the lower class again, as was Hilary's, which made her furious.

Even though having Hilary in the lower class consoled me, it was hard not to feel like I'd done something wrong. Most girls who placed higher were returning students, but I fixated on the two new girls who went straight to the upper level.

Every decision seemed to carry significance about my future as a dancer. I tried to convince myself it was OK if I made it to the upper class by the following year.

At least my favorite teacher from the summer was teaching my first class. Vivienne was the most human. She was the only one who was married with kids.

When I walked in, Hilary was by the studio door, studying her reflection in the mirror. Once school started, she would always beat me there in the morning. I'd only have thirty minutes to run five blocks from YAH to make it to ballet on time.

I felt a tinge of jealousy. When Hilary worked on her correspondence courses in the morning, she wouldn't have to leave our room.

I walked across the room to claim a barre spot on the other side.

Barre spots on the first day were crucial. Dancers were territorial; after the first day, we'd probably all stand in the same places. I carefully staked out my position: somewhere inconspicuous and not in the teacher's face. During the summer, there was an urgency to make the teacher notice me since I was angling for the year-round invite. But now, I wanted to hide.

At home in Rock Island, my barre spot had an unobstructed view of my reflection. There was a comparable spot in the back of the studio. I grabbed it.

The room filled up. The returning students were louder than us new kids, catching up with each other after being away the entire summer. I sat down to put on my pointe shoes. We weren't allowed to wear ballet slippers in the upper division. It was pointe shoes all the time, every class, just like dancers with real jobs in Ballet New York.

What if I was the worst dancer in the class, and SBNY decided they'd made a mistake? I felt a wave of homesickness. The familiarity of my old studio felt so far away.

A girl I'd noticed sitting alone in the cafeteria at breakfast took the spot in front of me. Her blonde hair was in an elaborately braided bun, and her high cheekbones and sculpted eyebrows gave off an air of sophistication. She seemed ill at ease, too.

I told her my name.

She introduced herself as Marie, with a French accent, rolling the *r*. I could hardly believe how beautiful she was, like a supermodel. She sat down in the frog position, knees bent and flat against the floor, the soles of her feet touching. We whispered for a few minutes, and I learned she was brand new to the school and hadn't been there for the summer course. She'd been at a ballet school in Paris and auditioned by video.

I stretched out in the middle splits and picked at my fingernails, hoping Marie would be a friend.

Vivienne swept into the room wearing a green leotard, black leggings, a black skirt, and pointe shoes. She was in her fifties and had a body like a twenty-year-old. Over the summer, I'd learned that she obsessed over the mechanics of ballet technique, and to her, executing a correct *tendu* was life or death.

A tiny, wrinkled older woman dressed in an arrangement of scarves took her place at the piano. She adjusted her music and settled on the bench.

At ten o'clock on the dot, Vivienne clapped three times. We put our left hands on the barre. The stern expression on Vivienne's face made me think of all the students she had taught over the years.

I glanced around the room, noticing I was the shortest in the class except for Marie.

Vivienne put us through our paces at the barre. The warmer my muscles grew, the more I calmed down. Thinking about perfecting the movements instead of everything else was a relief.

After forty minutes, we came to the center. Once Vivienne divided us into two groups and we had the chance to watch each other, the competitive energy grew. We stood there and evaluated each other.

Hilary placed herself front and center. That confidence she'd had on display during the summer was back in full force, and the returning students looked at her and exchanged knowing glances. Nicole, the RA who'd checked me in on the first day, looked the most irritated.

From what I'd gathered from the boys, Nicole had been the class star the year before.

I guessed what was going through Nicole's head. She'd staked Hilary out as competition, rightly so. Hilary was a shade taller than her, but she had longer legs. They had similar short torsos and beautiful feet. Hilary was hyperflexible, like a Gumby doll, and could lift her leg higher than anyone in every direction. Nicole wasn't quite as flexible. Her legs had more strength, and she had a stunning *arabesque*. Hilary fit all the school's physical criteria, but Nicole knew the Roizman style and precisely what the teachers wanted.

Marie stood in the front line of the second group. She didn't need to be pushy to stand out; her beautiful face drew my eye. Our body types were similar. My feet and extension were better than hers, but her upper body was much more refined. She had excellent control over her movements and a commanding demeanor.

It felt good to dance, even with the tension, or maybe because of it. I focused on applying Vivienne's corrections. One problem dawning on me was that my arms needed a lot of work. Back in Rock Island, my ballet teacher never said anything specific about how to hold my upper body.

Vivienne had precise directions for how the hands and arms should always be.

It felt much safer to stay inconspicuous in the second line of the second group. There was so much new information to absorb. Like in any ballet class, we instinctively began to understand our roles in the group hierarchy. I was not the best, but not the worst, and a feeling of belonging took shape.

After the final leaps across the floor, we curtsied to show our respect. It was a reminder that dancing at this elite school was the height of privilege.

When I lifted my head from the bow, I noticed a shadow and felt a chill run down my spine. Every pair of eyes darted to our new audience.

Victor Caldwell, the artistic director of Ballet New York, stood silhouetted in the doorway. I was awed by the imposing sight of him, his brown hair smooth against his head and face chiseled like a movie star.

My first real-life glimpse of Victor Caldwell filled me with desperation. I knew why I was in New York, in this studio. I had come to learn how to be a professional ballerina—seeing him crystallized the goal and made my desired path concrete. I had to get into BNY, or I would *die*.

"Class dismissed," Vivienne announced, breaking the spell. She exchanged a polite nod with Victor.

"He must have stopped by the school for a meeting," Nicole whispered. "Most days, he's either on the 11th floor for company class and rehearsals or at the theater."

We applauded politely and disbanded to pick up our bags and clear the studio. Victor left.

I walked into the hallway and watched his figure disappear down the hall.

There were expectations at Young Artist's High. The school accommodated our hectic dance schedule but demanded academic excellence. Math, chemistry, and social studies were all harder than they'd been at my old high school. Because I was a social learner and had always taken school seriously, I quickly realized that YAH had been a good choice. My English teacher led engaging discussions, and there was no way I could have learned French on my own without a teacher in the room. Without YAH, obtaining a high school diploma would have been impossible with SBNY's demands.

Hilary's choice to do correspondence meant she would get her GED instead, and I could soon see that hers was a lonelier route. By junior year, when a professional contract was at most two or three years away, we didn't have time for anything resembling everyday teenage life. The more it sunk in how unusual our existence was, the more I was grateful for the three hours a day I spent in school.

YAH was five blocks from SBNY. When the weather was nice, I loved the walk outside, but by December, I was miserable running back and forth in the cold and snow. Marie swore in French all the way there and back.

Back home in Rock Island, I'd warmed up for thirty minutes before dance class, but in New York, there was only a half-hour between my morning French lesson and ballet. During that time, I ran the five blocks back to my dorm room, changed my clothes, took the elevator down to the ballet school, and shoved on my pointe shoes. I wore my hair up for school because I didn't want to lose a moment of that half-hour. Transitioning from a zero-degree snowstorm to executing *pliés* in only leotards and tights was physically excruciating. The SBNY dress code forbade leg warmers or sweaters in class. I knew the teachers needed to see every inch of our bodies, but I was constantly freezing during barre.

As the routine set in, days passed so fast that I lost track of time. I made a few casual friends at YAH outside of SBNY. The dancers stuck together in a clique, as did the movie actors, models, Broadway stars, and musicians, but I was one of the few ballet students who said hello to non-dancers. Most people talked to the same people at YAH as they did at SBNY.

Our academic classes were small, and whenever I had a moment where I wanted to lean more into school or non-dance friends, the environment and the structure of my life pulled my focus back to my career. My peers' behavior constantly reinforced that ballet was the priority. Not academics, not socializing, and not dating. That was just the way it was.

We were most comfortable with the people who practiced the same art form, and at the end of the day, there was no impetus or need to expand our social skills.

Hilary and I rarely went to meals or left the dorm together, but we still spent a lot of time with each other in our room. I met more people than she did because I went to school, but she was the one I brushed my teeth with before we went to bed. I wanted to like her, and part of me wanted to be like her, but when she said negative things about other people—which was all the time—I couldn't stand her.

One Saturday afternoon in late September, I returned from lunch in the cafeteria and found Nicole hanging out in our room. There had been subtle signs that Hilary and Nicole were becoming friendly despite how they competed. Like Marie and I did, they often talked while putting on their pointe shoes.

"We're going for frozen yogurt," Hilary said. "Want to come?"

It was the first time she'd invited me anywhere but the cafeteria, and I had barely talked to Nicole since the first day. The connection made me feel good. All I wanted was to hang out together and act like friends. We were always so intense in ballet class.

Outside, Hilary, Nicole, and I headed north on Columbus Avenue. The fall air blew across our cheeks and turned them pink. Hilary and Nicole walked fast, and keeping up or following their conversation was hard. We maneuvered around a steady stream of people on the sidewalk. They were gossiping about other dancers. I watched their perfect posture and long ponytails and wished I felt as confident as they looked.

After we'd bought our frozen yogurts from a window kiosk, Hilary said, "Unbelievable," in an outraged tone, loud enough for the older woman behind the window to hear. "I asked her to put sprinkles at the bottom of the cup. Sprinkles. Not sprink-le. How can I go on under these conditions? Where do they find these people?"

"That's where the Dolly Dinkle dancers end up working," Nicole said in a cutting voice. "If we don't get into a company, we could end up serving frozen yogurt someday, too."

"I'll buy my yogurt from you two once I get into BNY," Hilary said.

Nicole laughed. "You mean when *I* get into BNY?"

There was an extended silence where I looked from one to the other and tried to understand all the layers of what they'd said. "Just think of all the free frozen yogurt." I managed after a minute, trying to smooth over the sharp edge of competition. Their banter had a subtext that made me nervous.

We walked slower on the way home. Their conversation filled my mind with dread.

"You're so cute, Little Mis Worried," Nicole said, pinching my cheek.

Hilary pinched my other cheek and said, "Isn't she, though?"

That's when I realized how insignificant I was to the two of them. Nicole and Hilary didn't see me as a peer, and they didn't see me as a competitor. I was just a small-town dancer who'd come to New York to make them feel superior.

The following week, Madame Sivenko spent class shredding my self-confidence. She criticized everything about me: my hairstyle, the angle of my chin, how fast I turned, and where I focused my eyes. We all craved corrections, but it was too much to take in. She was on the attack for some unknown reason and determined to teach me a lesson.

"She hates me," I whispered to Marie, turning my face to the barre to blink back tears.

"Don't take it personally," Marie said. "She probably thinks you're too nice and wants to toughen you up."

A minute later, Madame Sivenko forced Marie's toes down as far they would go in *tendu*. Marie winced when Madame Sivenko said, "Could you *bother* to point your foot?"

"She thinks you're too pretty and doesn't want you to rely on your looks," I told Marie over lunch later. We laughed, but we were both despondent.

A month into the school year, I walked into the studio for morning class and found Hilary standing at my usual spot at the barre. I froze in the middle of the room, confused. She deliberately ignored me, stretching innocently, examining herself in the mirror. She smoothed her red hair into her bun.

Marie looked at me as if to say, "I didn't know what to do." The other girls exchanged nervous looks.

What was Hilary's problem, anyway? She called her parents from the street most of the time, but the night before, I'd heard her on the phone in the hallway, and she'd shouted, "You don't understand anything. I hate you!" After I'd heard her yell, I felt sorry for her until she returned to the room and turned the lights off on me while I was reading in bed.

I glanced around, deciding what to do. If I took Hilary's usual spot, I'd have to stand at the front of the room. I didn't want to do that, especially since Madame Sivenko was teaching. I'd take another person's spot if I tried to stand elsewhere. I knew it was a joke, like when Hilary messed up my alphabetized CDs, but Hilary's tests weren't funny to me. They were mean.

Madame Sivenko walked into the room. I hurried to my usual spot and pushed between Hilary and Marie as if Hilary wasn't there.

"Can't you see there isn't space here?" Hilary said.

"My eyes work fine," I said, putting on my pointe shoes and tying the ribbons as fast as possible. The pianist settled at the piano, and Madame Sivenko clapped her hands for us to begin.

Hilary and I practically stood on each other through the first fifteen minutes. We needed more space to execute the combinations and constantly knocked arms and legs.

Madame Sivenko gave us a few curious looks. Finally, after she saw Hilary kick me in the face during *fondus*, she said, "What is going on here? Hilary, you should go stand in your usual barre spot."

In a syrupy voice, Hilary said, "I was trying to give other people a chance to stand in front, but I guess they didn't want to." She walked to her old place as if she deserved a medal, cementing the rivalry.

A frigid silence descended on our dorm room after that. After a few days, I tried to act like nothing happened. I couldn't sustain the tension.

Eventually, we eased into guarded small talk, but I couldn't shake the sense that she was out to get me.

My feet hurt all the time, in and out of pointe shoes. SBNY didn't allow ballet slippers in the upper division, the constant reminder that dancers in most professional ballet companies wore pointe shoes all day, every day. We had no choice but to learn to endure it, too. My feet alternated between feeling numb and on fire, and sometimes, daggers of pain raced up my legs. When I took my shoes off at the end of the day, sometimes I could barely walk.

"In Rock Island, I only wore these two hours a day at most," I complained to Marie before class one morning. "This is excruciating."

"Four to six hours a day is a big change for me, too," she commiserated.

"At least when I'm dancing, I can sometimes forget," I said, standing and checking the wall clock. "But this is awful, having to shove our cold feet into the shoes."

Madame Sivenko would be there any minute.

Marie applied lip gloss and said, "I think it's worse after we take them off and see our toes bleeding."

"We can do this," I said. "Remember, we're supposed to look happy in them."

Class began and took our minds off the pain. The work was more important.

But when we took our shoes off together at the end, blood and pus caked the right foot of Marie's tights. I'd developed corns between my two littlest toes, which hurt like a . . . I looked from Marie's face to her foot and back to her face, watching the tears rise in her eyes. She made me feel less alone.

"That looks horrible," I said.

Her eyes locked on mine. "I can't do this anymore."

I tried to joke. "Let's cut that foot off."

She said, "I am far too important in the world to spare a toe," and snapped her pointe shoe ribbons at me. "This foot could be worth millions. Have a little respect."

We hobbled out of the studio together.

Our toes formed blisters and bled all the time, but I made it a goal to go without any lamb's wool or padding and put them on as comfortably as sneakers. The more my feet hurt, the more determined I became.

Hilary's solution to her foot pain involved soaking her feet in a bucket of ice water at night. She'd put her feet in the freezing pail and wail, looking for sympathy. I sewed pointe shoes at my desk and ignored her.

There was nothing like the ritual of a new pair. Preparing them was an elaborate process: sewing on elastics and ribbons, cutting the satin off the outside of the toe box, darning the edges around the toe, bending the stiff shank that reached from heel to toe under the foot, spraying the shank with shellac to make it last, gently closing the door hinge on the toe box to soften it, and then strengthening the inside of the toe using an entire tube of super glue. After finishing all the steps, I dried them overnight on the radiator.

One night, I wore an old pair of pointe shoes to bed. "Maybe this will toughen up my feet," I said.

Hilary watched me in disbelief and said, "You're crazy."

"It's just an experiment."

Later that night, I woke up screaming and ripped the shoes from my feet. It hurt. It hurt *so much.*

Foot pain aside, my body's inadequacies bothered me more than any pair of pointe shoes. Physical pain was nothing compared to mental anguish. When I received a correction in class, I had difficulty sustaining the change for longer than a few minutes. There was so much to think about. My brain wanted to bend my body to my will, but more often than not, my limbs did the very thing the teacher said was incorrect.

"You're smarter than this," Madame Sivenko said after I messed up the *petit allegro* right in front of her. She made me repeat the jump combination alone without music. My classmates watched critically.

"How can you let your rear stick out like that?" she said when I finished. "No wonder you can't get off the ground."

I didn't cry, not then. I sobbed in the shower at the end of the day. In private, I could let my angst flow out like a balloon letting out air. The steam, the physical suffering, and the humiliation of having all my flaws pointed out swirled around me.

If our first class of the day ended a minute early, we huddled in the doorway of the Advanced Men's class. We sized up which boys we wanted to partner with. *Pas de deux* class didn't start until a few weeks into the year, but partnering was on everyone's minds. Watching the boys, I wondered why there were so many misconceptions about them.

Behind the scenes, the men held all the power, and I didn't understand why anyone would mock them. Girls had to be better looking and much more flexible. Boys didn't have to wear pointe shoes, and because they outnumbered us, they were in much higher demand.

Tyler executed an explosive leap at the front of the room. "He's a child prodigy," I said. "Victor must love him."

"Boys that talented are so rare," Marie agreed. "He has a big future with BNY."

"I can't believe he's only fifteen," I said.

Like many others, Tyler's body was lean and muscular, but his presence elevated him far above the others. When we'd met that first day in the cafeteria, I'd hoped I might be someone special to him, but once school settled into a routine, I realized he was the kind of person who seemed like everyone's best friend.

"The teachers always make him stand in the front," I said.

"He's so humble about it, too," whispered Marie.

They finished their final jump combination, and the music stopped. Tyler lingered in front and bent his knees with his right foot pressed to his left foot. He jumped, spinning twice with his legs tightly crossed, landing in the same starting position: a flawless double *tour en l'air*. He was lost in that zone where he was dancing; all that mattered were the steps.

The others examined themselves in the mirror. Simon was leaning on the piano and studying the students. Tyler looked to him for a reaction, and Simon made a small gesture with his hand, indicating that Tyler should bring his heels forward as he rotated his hips. Simon withheld approval, but Tyler nodded, knowing the correction was a compliment.

"Charlie is so awkward," Marie said. "Why does he always draw attention to himself when he messes up?" A moment after she said it, Charlie threw his arms in the air, rolled his eyes, and stomped off the floor.

"I'm such a loser," Charlie mumbled to himself.

Another presence was a Chinese boy named Qi. He was stocky with good technique and impeccable manners.

"You can tell Qi did martial arts," Marie whispered.

"His jump is good," I said, thinking Qi had a way of fading into the background. I'd tried to ask him a question in the cafeteria, but his broken English made the conversation difficult. When Simon corrected him, he looked grateful enough to cry.

Marie said, "I think Jamal has so much promise." I smirked, knowing that she meant she had a crush on him. Jamal was the tallest and most grown-up-looking, with eyes and skin like dark chocolate cake. He had a unique movement quality, and we'd discussed more than once how he had a wicked sense of humor underneath his tough exterior.

There was one more we stared at. "Jesse is smoking hot, and he knows it," Marie said. Jesse was tall and well-built but only a decent dancer. I'd been surprised to discover that his jumps and turns were passable at best. His eyes constantly darted to the door to check who was watching him.

Marie said, "It's funny how Jesse is so confident everywhere but in the studio. We make him nervous."

CHAPTER 4

As I walked toward the elevator after pointe class, the woman at the front desk waved me over. She asked if I wanted a ticket to see Ballet New York that night.

"We get to go to the opening night gala for free?" I asked. That couldn't be true.

"The school wants you to go to as often as possible," she said, using her pointer finger to push her glasses up her nose. "How else will you get to see the professionals at work?"

A group gathered in the lobby after dinner and walked across the plaza together. As we reached the fountain, Tyler came up next to me. "You clean up good," he said, and his hand brushed my hair. "Let me see where you're sitting."

My heart pounded when I handed the ticket to him. There was nervous energy between us, going out at night and standing in the cold air. He said our seats were together.

After we'd walked through the lobby and passed the usher, he took me by surprise by taking my hand. He ignored the other kids. We might as well have been the only two people there. It felt like a date as he led me down the aisle to our seats.

The lights dimmed before we had time to talk. I settled in as the musicians took their positions and the conductor bowed. We clapped. The conductor raised his baton, and the orchestra played the overture.

"You look like you're enjoying this," he whispered in the middle of the first ballet.

I'd forgotten he was there. How had I never known beauty like this existed? What we did in class was work. The shows I'd done at home had been fun. But this! Ballet New York on stage was magic. I'd never seen anything like it.

"That could be you up there in another year or two," he said a few minutes later, and I'd never felt so vulnerable or so seen. His breath was warm against my neck. My stomach flipped over, but I fixed my eyes on the stage.

He touched my knee and said, "This is fun seeing it through your eyes. Most of the other girls are used to it."

When the curtain fell at the first intermission, I turned to him and said, "It's rude to talk during the performance."

"Arrest me," he said with a smile. "But before that, tell me what you thought. Did you see Pamela Davies fall out of line in the third movement? They should fire her."

I said, "I have so many questions. How do they remember such complicated choreography?"

We talked straight through both intermissions. There was so much to say that we continually interrupted each other.

From that night forward, Tyler and I fell into a pattern of attending performances together. Hilary invited herself with us once, but she was the third wheel and knew it. Because we were performance buddies, it felt natural when he became my regular partner in *pas de deux* class.

There were many Roizman ballets that I didn't know about and could never have seen in Rock Island. I had a new identity and clear purpose when I sat in the audience, excited for the next performance. Every show was both a pleasure and research for my future.

We saw Victor Caldwell in the audience occasionally. "He watches from backstage a lot of the time," Tyler said.

Victor would slip into his seat in the house just as the lights went down, and my eyes would track him every time.

"I swear he looked at you," Tyler whispered, knowing how much Victor's presence prickled the hair on the back of my neck.

I pushed my knee against his. "I think he had something in his eye."

After we'd been to a few shows together, Tyler invited me to hang out in his room if I didn't have too much homework. He didn't have a roommate. The boys were lucky because they all had singles. His room was a flight of stairs below mine, on the boys' floor, which was always a mess.

I followed him into the suite he shared with Jesse, Charlie, and Jamal. The other doors were closed, and they were nowhere to be seen. He did a chin-up on the bar across his doorway.

After I walked into his room, he shut the door, even though the rule was that doors stayed open when we had visitors. The room smelled like my dad's deodorant and clean laundry. "You're so clean for a boy," I said. There were textbooks and notebooks piled neatly on his desk. Posters of classic rock bands decorated the walls.

"I like to keep things organized," he said.

His black and yellow Pittsburgh Steelers hoodie hung over the back of his desk chair. He always wore it to breakfast. Feeling bold, I picked it up and put it on. "I'm cold," I explained, and he smiled and stared at me.

"Yesterday's performance was better, don't you think?" He pushed his school stuff on the floor so I could sit on his bed. "Diana had an off night."

"You think?" I asked, taking a seat cross-legged on his beige comforter. "I don't think she ever has an off night."

"Everyone does," he said. He lay on the floor beside the bed and stared at the ceiling.

I said, "You're so lucky. You've learned all this by osmosis. Most of what I know comes from ballet books instead of experience. I wish I knew as much as you did."

"You remind me of my sister," he said. "She's why I got into dance, and she still romanticizes it. It's so weird that I'm the one who ended up here. She quit after I moved out."

I'd always wanted a sibling and thought how strange it would be to come here and leave one behind. I wondered if his sister was proud or resented his success.

We studied each other. He kicked off his shoes and flexed his feet. Even with his dress pants on, I could see all the muscles flexing in his legs. Watching him stretch was hypnotizing.

"Why did your parents let you leave home so early?" I asked. "Twelve is so young."

"I don't even know. We don't have much money, and they both work a lot. It was something I wanted. They thought it was a good opportunity." He propped himself up on his elbow and held my gaze.

Something told me he rarely talked about himself, so I listened.

"I want my family to be proud of me," he announced, eyes penetrating mine. "But I get lonely. It's hard." He shifted onto his back, folded his hands behind his head, and stared at the ceiling. The depth of his feelings permeated the room.

We'd become touchy-feely with each other the last few weeks, arms around each other's shoulders or holding hands, and I considered getting on the floor and putting my arms around him.

He'd made himself vulnerable, and what had been fun between us before now felt dangerous. As we sat there in silence, an invisible bubble grew around him. As much as I knew he liked being near me, he gave off an unspoken energy that only let me get so close.

We listened to music for a while, and then I said goodnight and returned to my room. It was so strange to have talked about something other than ballet.

I was getting to know the SBNY Tyler better, but the real Tyler, the one no one could see underneath his perfect *pirouettes*, felt farther away than I'd realized. He was like something beautiful I could only admire on a stage.

"My parents are very strict," Marie said. We were on our walk back to YAH after lunch. "They expect me to be very driven, and I know how much they sacrifice for me. They moved to a smaller apartment to save money so I could come to SBNY."

I took in that information. It sounded like a lot of pressure. "Why didn't you go to ballet school in Paris?"

"French ballet is fine, but we prefer the Roizman style. When I was thirteen, we saw Ballet New York on tour, and my parents decided I should come here."

I wondered if that meant she hadn't gotten into the school in Paris. "Fine? French ballet is *fine*?"

"Don't be so provincial," she said, teasing.

"Don't be such a snob."

We grinned at each other.

"Don't misunderstand," she said after a minute. "The French respect ballet much more than Americans do. We bend nature to man. That is why France has so many beautiful gardens and incredible architecture. You Americans let nature run wild. Just look at all your national parks."

That made me think. Ballet was a little of both structure and natural beauty. We had to be so disciplined. For example, my back had a natural tendency to sway. I had to figure out from the inside how to shape it back into the straight spine that's required for proper ballet lines. The problem was that it felt so good to let my back sway. It was so easy to let my muscles go, relax, and let my body remain as it naturally was. A swayed back was not beautiful, though. Not ballet beautiful. Not perfection.

Tyler and I went to see *Elements*, a ballet in three acts I'd read about but had never seen in real life.

"Why does *Elements* only have three sections: *Earth*, *Wind*, and *Fire*?" I asked, settling in my seat. "What happened to *Water*?"

Tyler put his jacket over the back of his chair and sat down. "When Roizman was choreographing *Elements*, the ballerina he planned to make *Water* for got pregnant," he said. "He was so angry that he cut the entire ballet."

My eyes grew wide. "Whoa."

We turned to watch the conductor approach the front of the orchestra pit.

The lights went down, and we clapped with the rest of the audience. After a brief overture, the curtain rose. A *corps* of ten girls wearing long gold tutus executed identical steps.

I experienced it almost without breathing. All my energy focused on the stage. Why did specific movements register, and others made no impact on me? The choreography was so intricate. Each dancer made delicate hand gestures, forming complex patterns together. I imagined how they felt at each moment.

My favorite dancers were the most self-aware. They translated their intentions into execution. What were they thinking about as they worked so hard?

Two-and-a-half hours later, the performance ended. We stood and stretched our backs, waiting for other patrons to file out. I was surprised to see Hilary with Nicole and Jesse on the other side of the orchestra section. She hadn't mentioned she was coming when I was getting dressed in our room.

Jesse didn't hang out with girls as much as Tyler and looked uncomfortable with how they were all over him.

Hilary talked loudly and gestured on one side of him, and Nicole leaned over him to hear her.

When they walked down the aisle, Hilary put her arms around Jesse's neck and whispered in his ear. Nicole grabbed his other hand and pulled him down the row, leaving Hilary behind.

I grabbed Tyler's hand and led him down our row in the opposite direction, avoiding them. We left the theater through a different door and ignored them as we passed them outside. I caught a flicker of irritation in Hilary's eyes.

We passed the Lincoln Center fountain on our way. The water glittered, colored by the interior lights. The plaza looked romantic, all lit up at night. Tyler put his arm around me.

I said, "Wasn't *Fire* amazing? "That *pas de deux* was the highlight of my week."

Diana Rampling and Richard Jackson had danced the leads that night. It was the kind of performance the dancers enjoyed. They took risks and made every movement fun while making it clear how deeply they thought about each step.

I couldn't stop thinking about Diana Rampling's beauty: tall, long, flexible limbs, dark hair, and those fantastic feet. Her impression haunted me, casting a long shadow over what I was and what I hoped to be. Richard Jackson epitomized masculinity with his powerful shoulders and partnering skills.

Tyler was lost in his own thoughts.

I couldn't read him. Tyler had been there for so long that he took the world-class quality of Ballet New York for granted. A sinking feeling came over me as I realized how childlike I sounded.

The performances increased my determination in a way that class never did. Even after thousands of classes, I was amazed that a human body could dance something as complex as *Fire*.

I *had* to make it. The ballets wouldn't exist without the dancers to do the steps. Almost every company member went through the school and earned their living dancing Roizman ballets. Why not me?

"Do you think I'll be tall enough for BNY?" I asked, saying the question out loud for the first time.

Tyler stopped and looked at me. I met his eyes, looking for an answer, but there wasn't one. "You're always worrying. Stop and try to enjoy the evening." He wrapped me in a hug, calming my anxiety.

After a minute, he pulled away. "We should dance *Fire* together," he said.

For a moment, lifted by his confidence, I could almost envision it.

"Do that again, Nicole," Madame Sivenko said Monday in class. She narrowed her eyes, and Nicole lit up with happiness. She loved corrections. A teacher's attention meant power.

"Eyes over the hand in *arabesque*," Madame Sivenko said matter-of-factly as she rose off her stool and approached Nicole, standing in the front line. Nicole was one of her favorites.

Madame Sivenko examined Nicole's starting position. Nicole angled her shoulders and hips at a diagonal in relation to the mirror. She stepped forward onto her right toe, her left leg rising high in the air straight behind her. She looked over her hand and stretched her right arm before her nose. Her left arm reached the left side, parallel to the floor. It was apparent why the teacher's eye had gone to Nicole—she had the most beautiful aesthetic line—but her balance was off, and she stumbled out of the *arabesque*.

"Chin higher," Madame Sivenko coached. "Let's see you hold the position."

Nicole tried and fell off her pointe again.

Hilary moved a little closer to Nicole. She crossed her arms in an intimidating way.

"Tighten your abdominals," Madame Sivenko instructed, eyes boring into Nicole. She waited for Nicole to readjust.

I glanced at the clock, conscious that this was taking away precious minutes of class time.

Nicole never had to try as hard as a lot of us because dancing came so naturally to her body. But our teacher's persistence sent the message: OK was not good enough. At SBNY, we didn't quit until we did it right. We were never allowed to assume that dancing would be easy. Even the most talented dancers could do more. We could always do more.

In the reflection, I studied the twenty-four other girls in black leotards, pink tights, and pointe shoes. My calves cramped, and I shifted into a stretch. We looked so much alike with our hair in buns.

We watched Nicole as if her body were our science experiment.

Collective resentment grew. The clock was ticking.

The rising tension put even more pressure on Nicole. Gritting her teeth, she stepped into *arabesque* again. This time, she stayed on balance. She looked at herself in the mirror when she realized she'd nailed it. She stayed there for one count. Two. Three. Four. Five. Six. Seven.

Before she came down, she lifted her back leg even higher in the air, a beautiful moment of extension and control that inspired awe. When she finally came off *pointe,* she smiled. Even the finish was extraordinary.

I had never seen a girl my age sustain an *arabesque* like that. The accomplishment took my breath away but tore me up inside. As much as I admired her perfection, I wanted to scream when I watched someone do so much more than I could.

Hilary immediately began practicing her *arabesque* next to Nicole. She balanced for a count or two, but Madame Sivenko didn't notice, and Hilary's features twisted in frustration.

"Well, you balanced," Madame Sivenko told Nicole. "But that wasn't what I asked for. I told you to keep your eyes over your hand and raise your chin. If I were Victor Caldwell, why would I want to hire someone who ignored my instructions? I could never trust you onstage. Your job is to follow directions."

She marched to the front and clapped her hands. The first group stepped forward to repeat the combination.

I hung in the back, frozen with frustration. How would I impress her if Madame Sivenko didn't appreciate it when Nicole executed such an extraordinary balance?

If all it took to succeed were the ability to look over your hand and raise your chin when Victor Caldwell asked, we'd all be in Ballet New York.

Jesse was drinking at the water fountain when we filed into the hallway after class. Nicole and Hilary raced over to hug him, pushing to get ahead of each other. I waited to get a drink until they moved out of the way.

The cold water felt good on my throat, and I drank and drank until my stomach was cramped. When I finished, I turned right into Jesse's chest. He towered over me. "Sorry." I backed up and bumped into the water fountain.

"How come you never say hi to me?" Jesse asked. His eyes were so gorgeous under those knitted, intense eyebrows.

My face heated up. Jesse and I ignored each other—I'd thought it was mutually understood. We'd never partnered in *pas de deux* class and had only eaten one meal together since the first day.

"Can't we be friends?" he asked.

It was the first time we made eye contact that way. I was startled by the intensity of how he looked at me. It wasn't bad, but it was new.

Tyler hugged me constantly, but the more Jesse stared into my eyes, the more I realized that Tyler rarely looked directly at me. We were comfortable together. Jesse made me uncomfortable.

I hurried away, irritated that I'd felt chemistry with him. He was too cocky for me and too much of a cliché. There had been enough good-looking guys back home who acted like they could have anything they wanted.

I walked into the cafeteria to get lunch before my afternoon French class, sensing the obsession over food that dominated the place. I still ate three daily meals, but the peer pressure in the dining hall made me feel guilty. Marie and I often talked about how messed up it was.

I stood in line behind Nicole and her mom, who looked like her. They were talking and didn't notice me. I'd seen her mom around because Nicole was the only girl in my class and the dorms whose family lived in Manhattan. Tyler said her parents were Upper East Side socialites who wanted her to have the same experience as the rest of the upper-division students.

"I'm not hungry," Nicole said.

"You must be, after all that exercise," her mom said.

"What do you know?" Nicole said. She stared at the French fries. Her expression sank into the zoned-out look she had many times in class.

"Excuse me," I said, reaching to take a bun for my veggie burger.

Nicole startled. "I didn't see you," she said.

Her mom turned and looked at me. "Are you in Nic's class?"

"Mom, this is Anna," Nicole said. "She's Hilary's roommate."

Her mom shook my hand. "I always like to meet Nicole's friends."

"Mom," Nicole said rudely, giving her a look. Her mother looked hurt.

Feeling embarrassed by their tension, I said, "You should have seen Nicole in class today. She hit the most amazing balance."

Her mom brightened. "That's so nice to hear. Sweetie, you didn't tell me."

But Nicole had walked away.

I headed toward the cash register, feeling homesick. After a glance back at the forlorn look on Nicole's mom's face, I found a seat and ate my veggie burger. A few minutes later, I walked outside and down Amsterdam Avenue toward YAH.

Pas de deux class on Fridays was the highlight of the week. The energy was so different from our all-girls classes. The room crackled with excitement.

Matthew Talroy, the soloist with BNY, was our teacher and the only one we had who was still dancing professionally. He was a great dancer and partner and younger and infinitely more approachable than Vivienne, Madame Sivenko, and Simon. Everyone loved his charming Alabama accent. From how he joked around with us, we knew he enjoyed the class as much as we did.

Matthew often called on me to demonstrate combinations as his partner because I was the shortest and smallest in the class. He gave me more attention than any of the other teachers, and I was popular with the boys, too, because of my size.

The Friday after the weird moment with Jesse, Matthew used me to demonstrate the first combination—mostly partnered *pirouettes*—for the rest of the class. I alternated between Tyler and Qi when we began dancing in groups.

"Faye's stuck with Charlie again," Marie whispered. We watched Charlie mess up the timing of a turn and dig his thumbs into Faye's ribs.

"I begged Tyler and Qi to grab me if they saw Charlie coming," I said.

"I did the same with Jamal," Marie said. "Poor Faye. It's because she still lives with her parents in Queens. If she lived in the dorms, the other boys would know her better and protect her."

"You and Jamal are so funny," I said.

"Why, because we're so different?" she asked.

I said, "You're so proper and polite, and when he talks, all I hear is 'yo,' followed by opinionated commentary on rap music."

We laughed and watched Nicole and Hilary compete for Jesse. They stood to the side and glared whenever he went with someone else.

A few minutes later, I walked off the floor after a combination with Qi. "Your turns very nice," he said, patting me on the shoulder.

Tyler grabbed my hand to repeat the step with him. I let him lead me into the opening *arabesque promenade.*

"Come on, Jesse," Hilary said, dancing on our left as the combination continued, "Eight turns."

Jesse exerted more energy into rotating her waist, and as we danced, I could feel the tension coming off them. They moved too close to us. She was frustrated that he wasn't doing what she wanted.

"Can you guys move over?" Tyler whispered politely, but Hilary danced even closer to me. Her pointe shoe slammed into my face as she opened her leg out into *arabesque*.

"Oww." I fell off pointe and stepped away from Tyler, bringing my hands to my eye. Hilary tried to keep dancing, but Jesse let go of her. Everything was blurry. The music petered out, and dancers moved closer to me to see what had happened.

"It was Anna's fault," Hilary said, glaring at me. "You shouldn't have been dancing on top of us."

"But you—" I started to say.

"You're bleeding," said Tyler. He touched my wrist, guiding my hand lower than my eye to touch the scraped skin on my cheek. My head ached.

"Can someone go for ice?" Matthew asked. Hilary just stood there.

Jesse said, "I'll do it," and left the room.

Matthew examined my face. "Are you okay?" he asked in his adorable accent.

"I'll just step out for a minute," I said.

Tyler guided me to the door, and class resumed as I left the studio.

I was tired of Hilary and her attitude. Why didn't anyone call her on her bad behavior?

Jesse met me on my way down the hall. He handed me an ice pack.

"It's okay," I said, brushing him away. "I'm fine." My head throbbed.

"No, you're not," he said, following me into the girl's bathroom.

Ignoring him, I splashed water on my face. When I finished, he handed me paper towels and pressed the ice to my cheek. I could only tolerate the cold for a minute before I pushed him away. In the reflection, I could already see an ugly bruise forming.

"Hilary is mean to you," Jesse said. Our eyes met in the mirror.

I avoided his eyes. "She's your friend."

"It's only because I'm a guy and tolerate her." He paused. "She's your roommate, but she's not your friend."

I turned to face him, leaning my back against the sink. "How would you know?" He wasn't as clueless as I'd thought.

"You're pretty, even with a black-and-blue cheek," he said, and his confidence did something to me. A shot of electricity sparked between us.

"We should get back," I said.

He smoothed a loose piece of my hair back into my bun, letting his fingers brush the back of my ear. His lips moved slowly toward mine.

No. That would make me as easy as every other girl in his life. He would never take me seriously. The kiss would turn into a joke he laughed about with the other guys, or worse, Hilary and Nicole.

I sidestepped him suddenly, and he fell forward into the sink. I charged out the door and down the hall.

"Wait," he called, hurrying to catch up.

"I'm not one of your groupies," I said over my shoulder. "I don't trust you."

Ignoring the hurt look on his face, I walked back into the studio, embarrassed. The class was almost over, and I stood in the back and watched the last combination. Tyler tried to cheer me up and asked me to dance twice, but my motivation was gone for the day. I was confused about Jesse, mad at Hilary, and dreading returning to my room for the evening.

Nicole took Jesse's hand and led him onto the floor. "You're so sweet, helping Anna like that," I heard her whisper as they danced. Matthew watched and corrected them at the end of the combination. They looked great together.

For all I knew, Jesse had already kissed Nicole.

Tyler leaned against the barre next to me. "We look better," he whispered, reading my mind.

CHAPTER 5

On a Sunday morning in late November, I sat outside on the ground in a corner of the plaza. It was cold outside, but I needed to be alone. I'd just seen the bulletin board and learned an established ballet school in New Jersey hadn't hired me for their annual production of *Nutcracker*. I was one of only eight students in the upper division not chosen. Most of my class would be in the show.

The New Jersey school always used SBNY students; their *Nutcracker* was a significant opportunity. It was a chance to perform in a semi-professional production, an annual tradition, and, let's face it, a status symbol.

Jen, one of the girls in the top class, came walking across the plaza. Her auburn hair was in a tight ponytail, and she had a determined look around her eyes. We'd never spoken, but everyone knew who she was, and by her nice outfit, I guessed she was on her way back from church. She was about five foot six, the perfect height.

She gave me a curious look. "Why are you crying?" she stopped to ask.

I said, "I'm OK," and wiped my eyes. "It's nothing."

"Of course. It's nothing." She made an exasperated sound and hugged herself to keep warm. "Sucks to cry over nothing. Most of the stuff they put us through isn't worth it."

I looked away. She sat on the ground next to me, and I worried she'd ruin her nice clothes. After a minute, I could see she wouldn't leave until I said more, so I told her I didn't get picked for *Nutcracker*.

"So what? It's just *Nutcracker*."

"They picked almost everyone else."

"If it makes you feel any better," she said, "I didn't get in last year when I was new and in the lower level."

A group of people who looked like college students walked past. We watched them for a while.

"I don't believe it," I said after considering what she'd said. She was practically perfect.

"Why?" she asked. "Because I'm in it this year? I served my time."

"Most of the students in my level haven't," I said.

Sometimes, it seemed like the teachers preferred the dancers who behaved like they didn't care. I was in class every day, working as hard as possible, but maybe that didn't matter. I longed for the days when I was the most talented girl back in Rock Island. I'd never be that person anymore.

Jen said, "Everyone here has problems; we're just experts at hiding it. That *Nutcracker* isn't even affiliated with SBNY. Who cares if they didn't pick you? You'll feel even more disappointed once Spring Workshop casting goes up. If you want to make it, you'll cry through worse disappointments." The wind whipped her hair across her face.

"What happens at Spring Workshop?" I asked, realizing I knew nothing about the end-of-year SBNY performance. It was hard to imagine feeling more disappointed than I did then.

Jen said, "The workshop is a huge deal. The *New York Times* reviews it every year. Artistic directors from the major companies come to scout dancers, and they often offer contracts after the shows."

That sounded like a fairytale. "Do we all automatically get to be in it?"

"This isn't your pay-to-play small-town recital," she said. "They only use the top class. You won't be in it this year. Of course, they need all the boys, but they only cast the girls who they think are ready for jobs."

I pulled my knees up toward my chest and hugged my legs. We sat for a while. The silence gave me space to think, and her companionship comforted me. "This is too hard."

"Everything worthwhile is hard," she said.

When I thought about what she'd said, I felt better. She was nice. "You look younger with your hair down," I said. "You almost look like a different person. In the studio—"

"We're all just bodies in there," she said.

They'd weeded out so many people already. Those left had bodies that fit the mold, but my body wasn't a machine. I was a flesh and blood young woman, still growing and changing.

"Forget about *Nutcracker*," Jen said. "They probably think you haven't picked up enough of the style yet. It's not the end of the world. You just got here."

I didn't know what to say.

She continued, "There are so many good things to do in New York—that I could never do back home in Colorado— and the best part is they have nothing to do with ballet. You need to get out more."

I agreed and stood, offering her a hand to help her up. We walked back toward the dorms together.

In the elevator, she said, "We're going to hang out. You can't spend too much time moping around like this. It's bad for you. Next weekend, we'll get half-price tickets in Times Square and see a Broadway show that makes us cry."

"I think I've cried enough." But it felt good to have something to look forward to besides taking classes and watching Ballet New York perform.

Jen reassured me that I didn't have to try so hard to impress everyone. She reminded me that the constant effort was too exhausting.

After we parted, I knocked on Tyler's door. He didn't answer, but I knew he was in because I heard noise in his room. I realized he was on the phone when I pressed my ear against the wood.

"I like you a lot, too, Jessica," I heard him say. "But this just isn't working. I'm only home during the summer. I can't be the kind of boyfriend you want."

My face turned warm. He'd never lied to me, but he'd never told me the truth, either.

There was a long silence. I held my breath. It wasn't like we'd ever kissed. He'd never mentioned he had a girlfriend. I shouldn't have eavesdropped, but I couldn't help myself, even as I realized the situation was precisely why I still avoided talking on the phone in the dorms.

Maybe he was breaking up with her because he liked someone else? After a while, when I grew more afraid of getting caught, I tiptoed away, feeling guilty that I knew something about him he hadn't wanted to share. Why was he even trying to have a long-distance girlfriend? Didn't he realize that everything that mattered in our lives was here?

I flew home to Rock Island for two weeks in December, right before the holidays. My mom was Christian, and my dad was Jewish, so we didn't do much for Christmas or Hanukkah, but it was nice to be home. My parents were in good spirits.

We went ice skating. "Tell me something," Dad said at the rink as we laced up our skates. "Are things OK with your roommate?"

"Why do you ask?" I said, not wanting to get into it. They kept asking me personal questions. I just wanted to tell them about my teachers and ballet, not my social life.

"We feel so out of touch with you now," Mom said, grabbing onto the rink's edge.

As we glided along the ice, I told them what I could, mostly a few facts about Marie, Jen, and Tyler.

My parents smiled knowingly at each other. I knew what they were thinking and vowed not to mention Tyler again.

"Do you do anything outside ballet?" Dad said. "Maybe you could fit in some volunteer work to enhance your college application."

He'd missed the point. Why was he thinking about college?

I said, "Don't be ridiculous."

My parents exchanged another look.

I threw my hands up in exasperation and skated away from them.

I dressed in a sparkly top and skirt on New Year's Eve and walked to Rachel's house. Her parents had agreed to let her have a party.

When I walked in the door, a few kids I didn't know well asked where I'd been and looked impressed when I told them I'd moved to New York for ballet.

Rachel hugged me and led me into the living room, where the most annoying kid we'd all tolerated since preschool was going around and shining his laser pen light into people's eyes. A good song played through the speakers. Kids turned the living room into a dance floor.

A cute boy I recognized from my eighth-grade English class caught my eye, and I wondered if he remembered me. He had brown hair and dimples, like Tyler.

Rachel and I worked our way into the center of the crowd and danced. The boy Rachel liked eyed her from the sidelines.

"You don't have to be a bunhead tonight," Rachel said, and we danced like the old after-school days when we'd hung out in each other's bedrooms, blasting our music and shouting the lyrics.

Rachel's crush came to dance with us.

"I'm tired," I said, winking at her before I walked away.

Someone crashed into me and spilled their drink down my shirt. We both apologized and the boy who looked like

Tyler took my arm to steady me. "This is so embarrassing," he said.

"It's fine," I said, although my top was soaked.

"I remember you," he said, "English class." He smiled.

He started to ask if I wanted to dance, but a girl I vaguely knew put her arm around him. "Thanks for keeping an eye on my boyfriend," she said with a pointed look.

I said, "I'm just heading home," and walked out the door. I hoped Tyler was thinking about me and wondered if he was with that girl in Pittsburgh. The Rock Island kids would continue their lives in such a different direction.

"Is my house still standing?" Rachel's mom asked when I pushed open my front door. She'd left Rachel's dad in charge of the party and walked over to say hi to my parents.

Dad stood and said, "You're home right in time to watch the ball drop. Want a sip of champagne?"

"Sure," I said, watching him pop the bottle open.

"Happy New Year," the crowd from Times Square shouted through the TV. We made a toast.

After a few more minutes, I was tired and said goodnight. While the rest of the world celebrated, I fell asleep dreaming of New York.

CHAPTER 6

"You still aren't separating your fingers," Vivienne told me the first week back in January. "You should carry your hand as if you have a diamond ring on each finger. What you need is a ball to make you aware of your placement. Get one and hold it during barre every day."

I took her words to heart, and the first thing I did on my way back to YAH was to stop at Rite Aid and buy a small squishy stress ball. Vivienne looked pleased when I brought it to her next class, and I continued to hold that ball at the barre for the rest of the year.

The significance of her lesson became clear many weeks later. I looked in the mirror and realized I was unconsciously holding my hand in a completely different and beautiful way. The hand shape she'd wanted me to master had become natural, and I hardly knew it was happening.

Audition tours began in the winter and early spring. The significant San Francisco, Seattle, Miami, Boston, and Houston schools came to recruit students for their six-week summer training programs, and I took all the auditions. San Francisco was my top choice. It felt like decades ago that I'd auditioned for SBNY in Chicago, but it had only been a year.

The companies affiliated with those schools held separate auditions.

"Are you doing any of the company auditions?" Jen asked. We were sewing shoes together in her room. "I should for the experience, but I only want Ballet New York and don't want to turn something down," she added.

That caught me off-guard. "This year? I'm not ready, and it's not like Ballet New York holds an audition since they only take students from SBNY. Why doesn't SBNY let us stay for the summer?"

She threaded a needle and said, "They need room to screen new students for next year."

In March, I received a letter from San Francisco. I sat at my desk after dinner and prepared to open it. What if everyone else got in and I didn't? At least the envelope was thick.

There was a knock on the door, and like always, Jen burst into the room before I could say to come in.

"Did you get it?" she asked.

"This?" I held up the envelope.

"Go on," she commanded.

I ripped it open. "Dear Anna Forester," I read, "we're pleased to inform you that you've been awarded a full scholarship to our summer program in San Francisco—"

She cheered.

I said, "Let's go together. We'll have so much fun."

Hilary appeared in the doorway and said, "I can hear you guys shrieking from down the hall."

"We're going to San Francisco," I said, happy enough that she didn't bother me.

"I'm sure Jen is," Hilary said.

Her implication felt like a gut punch. I said, "I got in, too."

"Where are you going this summer, Hilary?" Jen asked.

"Home to Pittsburgh," Hilary said. "I got a scholarship to San Francisco, but my parents are making me go home for the summer." She kicked off her shoes and hopped on her bed, stretching her legs out in front of her. "My feet hurt. And my hip hurts."

Jen and I exchanged a look. "Let's go see if Marie's letter came," I said, following Jen out of the room.

We paused in the hallway while I double-checked to make sure I had my key.

"I can't believe *she* got into San Francisco," we heard Hilary say to no one on the other side of the door.

Jen just looked at me.

I felt sick.

"She has problems," Jen said. "Her parents must know it if they're making her stick with a local summer intensive."

When Jen and I arrived, Marie held her acceptance letter up. Her room was straight out of a magazine ad—designer comforter, fresh flowers in the windowsill, expensive perfume and lotion on a mirrored tray. I'd never had a friend whose parents invested so much money in their child.

"Are we all going to San Francisco?" Marie asked.

Jen said, "Want to get an apartment together?" She studied the dresses hanging in Marie's closet. "Marie, you have the nicest clothes," she murmured. After a pause, she added, "My dad has a college friend in San Francisco who I bet would sublet his condo. He and his wife travel every summer. It's right on Van Ness."

"I'm very particular about my space," Marie said, "I've always had a single here—"

"You don't want to live in the dorms there, do you?" I asked. "Jen says she knows how to cook."

"I make fat-free pizza," Jen said.

"Ugh," I said, tired of hearing fat-free. "I'll order in."

"I can make crêpes," Marie said, warming to the idea.

We sat around her room planning for another hour, and by the time I left to get ready for bed, I was in the best mood. When I opened my door and flipped the light on, I couldn't even process what Hilary had done.

The desks and dressers had been moved to block off Hilary's side of the room. She'd piled books and extra pointe shoes high on the desk shelf to create a wall, and the TV on the dresser had been turned away from my side to face her bed. There was only a tiny opening by the closets for her to squeeze through.

I stared at her barricade, too shocked to say a word.

We weren't friends, but I hadn't seen this coming. I peeked around the desk to confirm she wasn't there. As I changed into my pajamas, I practiced what to say to her when she returned. Confused and hurt, I crawled into bed, turned the lights off, and waited.

Close to midnight, Hilary opened the door, flipped the lights on, and walked into the room with Nicole, laughing. I sat up, half-asleep. Nicole took one look at me and said goodnight.

After Nicole left, Hilary hurried to her side of the room. I jumped out of bed and followed her, overwhelmed with anger.

"Don't I get an explanation?" I demanded, putting my hands on my hips.

"Quit acting like we're friends just because I got stuck being your roommate," she said, her tone calm as she took her earrings out. "Everyone thinks you're so nice. I don't want anything to do with you. Now get out of here. You're not allowed on my side."

It was the first time someone flat-out said they didn't like me right to my face, and I was speechless.

"You're such a baby," she said. "I'm not talking to you anymore."

I backed away and went to my bed. She turned on the TV full blast, and, especially because I couldn't see the screen, the sideways glow of it bothered me as much as the sound.

"Turn it down," I said, but she ignored me.

I put my face on the pillow, feeling so sad I couldn't remember why I'd been happy a few hours earlier.

It took forever to fall asleep.

I called home early in the morning.

"It's six a.m.," Dad said. Mom was snoring in the background.

I said, "I hate it here. Why did you let me come? My roommate is the meanest person in the world. I'm so miserable. Please let me come home." I cried until my eyes hurt. Dad waited, letting me cry it out.

Finally, he said, "Come home then. We'd love it."

"I quit." It felt good to say it.

"Good," he said. "We could use your help with the laundry. Maybe you could even get a job at McDonald's. I'll teach you to mow the lawn."

"Dad," I said, so frustrated that I kicked the wall.

"I mean it," he said. "You can quit whenever you want."

He waited until I finished my meltdown and told me they loved me. We hung up. I walked to school.

Hilary and I didn't speak for almost two months, and as the school focused on the annual Spring Workshop, everyone was stressed and busier than ever. Madame Sivenko and Vivienne each staged a Roizman ballet, and a guest choreographer from the company choreographed an original piece.

In Rock Island, I always had the leading role in the spring recital. I was so sad watching all the girls in the class above prepare for the performance. Jen had a soloist role, and I tried to live vicariously through her. But she wasn't around as much because of rehearsals, and neither were the boys. I had more schoolwork. There was less time for friends.

"I feel bad for the seniors who don't have jobs yet," Tyler said as we walked home after a performance. We'd both been so busy. It was the first time we'd made it to the theater or hung out in weeks. "There's about ten of them. After the auditions, many girls still had nothing, and SBNY will make them leave in June. This is a bad year. Directors said they didn't have openings. At least some of the directors come to the show and occasionally change their minds if they like a dancer more onstage."

"They're lucky to have Workshop as a second chance," I said, twirling to watch my pink skirt fan out. "Dancers from other places only had one shot at auditions."

"They can't even try out for BNY," Tyler said.

I popped a mint in my mouth and offered him one. "Did any of the seniors decide on college?"

He laughed and said, "Decide isn't the right word."

By the time the Workshop happened in late May, after months of watching the upper class rehearse, I couldn't wait for the year to end.

When the big day arrived, Marie and I sat in the audience, curious to see the other students onstage for the first time. Performances revealed things about them we couldn't see in the studio. There was so much pressure to put a lifetime of work into one make-or-break performance.

"Next year, that'll be us," Marie said.

"I hope so," I said, but it felt far away.

She examined a perfectly manicured nail done at the salon up on Broadway and said, "Next stop, apprenticeships with BNY."

My nails were chewed to the quick. "If Victor likes us," I whispered. "He's never even taught our class."

She had more confidence than I did. "He will next year."

During intermission, I stood and scanned the audience. "Look who else is here besides Victor. William Mason from the Los Angeles Ballet Theater, Charles Diamond from Ballet San Francisco, and Bruce Pollock from the National Ballet Theatre. That's directors from four of the top companies in the country."

We squeezed hands to calm each other as the lights came down. Marie said, "Sit. Jen's next."

Jen performed the soloist role in a ballet called *Afternoon Symphony*. From what I'd seen peeking in the door at the top class, Jen could be reserved in the studio. To my surprise, she was a total extrovert onstage, smiling her heart out. Her technique was solid and precise. The choreography played to her strength—jumping—and she breezed through the steps.

Jesse, Jamal, Tyler, and the only Black girl in the upper division danced a *pas de quatre* in a new piece by one of the BNY principal dancers. The choreography was meh, and Jesse, Jamal, and the girl were fine, but Tyler was the standout. Of course. When he led his partner forward for their *pas de deux*, they commanded the stage enough to make the audience clap.

He confidently partnered her through her slow *developpés* and *promenades*, the exact steps he'd practiced with me in class every week. The girl had legs for miles and extensions up to her ears. They executed an impressive press lift, where he held her over his head in an *arabesque* pose, one leg extended behind her, his arms straight and strong as he walked her around the stage. He was a perfect partner: humble and attentive, making her look better than she did alone. The applause went on forever when they finished.

She ran offstage, and Tyler danced. He stole the show with his solo variation. His turns, *tours en l'air*, and leaps showed a mastery far beyond his sixteen years. The cheering and bravos went on for the longest time.

Later, when I congratulated him outside the stage door, Tyler said that Victor had come backstage and offered an apprenticeship to the gorgeous Black girl Tyler danced with. Tyler and Jen had been overlooked, but Tyler was unconcerned.

"Victor doesn't think I'm ready yet," Tyler said, far less outraged than I was. "I still have two more years of high school. I'd be the youngest one in the company if he takes me next season."

Like me, Jen had one more year of high school left, but she was devastated. To add to her misery, Ballet San

Francisco's director hired two girls and another boy after the Workshop performances.

The day after the show, we went to our favorite nearby café for chocolate mousse cake. For someone who acted so tough and above the competition, Jen was as vulnerable to disappointment as the rest of us. I had never been the one comforting her before.

"Madame Sivenko let me think I'd get into BNY," she said, digging her fork into the cake as if she wanted to kill it.

"You're one of the best dancers in the school," I said. My words were useless. The slight was so much bigger than me.

She said, "I asked Vivienne what happened, and she said Victor thinks my shoulders are too broad and my chest is big. She told me to do something about it over the summer, and I could repeat the upper division for senior year." With that, she pushed the plate at me.

"What exactly are you supposed to do?" I asked. I felt scared. What was I supposed to do if Victor decided I was too short? I didn't dare say how happy I was that we'd be in the same class together in the fall.

After a long silence, I asked, "Do you want to room together next year?"

"One hundred percent," she said. "Unless you want to room with Hilary again."

June arrived, and the city turned hot and humid. YAH ended, too, but there was one significant hurdle left before the year-round students departed: our end-of-year conferences.

"They always kick a few people out," Marie said. "I'm so relieved I'm not one of them." We were on the plaza, racing to finish our frozen yogurt before it melted. Her conference had been unremarkable, or at least that was what she told me, and they'd moved her up.

The school had canceled our afternoon classes during the last week, and I had fifteen minutes before I met with Madame Sivenko.

After Marie and I made plans to go shopping in the afternoon, I walked inside and took the elevator to the school floor. Madame Sivenko's office door was closed. I sat in the big leather chairs in the waiting area, wondering if she would recognize me with my hair down and in jeans and a T-shirt instead of leotards and tights.

Madame Sivenko's door opened, and Hilary walked out. Her red hair was hanging down over her face. She'd been crying.

"Are you OK?" I asked. I felt sympathy for her and more fear than ever.

"Stop staring at me," she said, genuinely upset.

"Next," Madame Sivenko called from inside the office.

Hilary paused and glanced back at the door. She fixed her green eyes on me. "They didn't kick me out if that's what you're wondering. She just told me I was turned in. Can you believe that?"

"For real?"

"Whatever," she said. "She still moved me up."

I admired her confidence. She walked toward the elevators.

My stomach was in knots, and suddenly, I didn't want to know what they thought of me. Walking into a room full of mirrors and other dancers daily took all the courage I had.

I took a deep breath and sat down in Madame Sivenko's office. The chair was so low that I had to crane my neck to see her over the desk.

Madame Sivenko pushed her gray hair behind her ears. With her hair cut so short, I couldn't imagine her as a ballerina back in the day. I wondered if the rumors that she'd had an affair with Roizman were true.

Her eyes appraised me over reading glasses I'd never seen her wear. "Let's have a look at your file." She opened a manila folder with my name written on it.

While she read silently, I studied the ballet manuals and videotapes on the shelves, the paintings of dancers on the walls, and the pigeon on the ledge outside the window. My heart was pounding so loud that I was sure she could hear it.

Without any emotion in her voice, she said, "Simon notes you have perfect attendance. Vivienne wrote, 'Anna has lots of potential but has not shown enough improvement.' I agree. You're too comfortable with technical habits from your previous training. We don't feel you grasp the Roizman style well enough yet."

I let the feedback sink in. Did Simon even know who I was? I'd been in his class twice a week for the entire year. What did that mean, that I hadn't improved enough? I was one of the hardest workers in the class. What else could I have done?

That was the first time I considered that I might be one of the dancers they kicked out of the school.

Wasn't it evident to them that the only thing that mattered in my life, the only thing I truly cared about, was ballet? I was never the girl that boys liked, the girl that played sports, the cool girl, the troublemaker. I was always the girl in motion, the girl who danced. I'd be lost without ballet.

Madame Sivenko looked at me. I was on the verge of tears. She sighed and said, "Work hard this summer. You must strengthen your pointe work to keep up in the higher class. Perhaps we haven't given it quite enough time."

She folded her hands together and rested them on the desk.

My mind was still racing. Had she moved me up? I'd never been so frustrated in my life. I always did my homework for school and received excellent grades. No matter how hard I worked at ballet, would I always only be mediocre?

"Go on now," she said, checking the clock. "We'll see you in September."

I walked down the hall, only mildly relieved. How didn't I meet their expectations? I was never injured and never missed a class. I held that ball in class for months to please Vivienne. Every minute I wasn't dancing, I thought about how to dance better the next time, and there wasn't one correction the teachers gave me that I didn't try my best to apply.

On Saturday morning, Vivienne taught my last class of the year. I was still upset and obsessing over my conference with Madame Sivenko.

At the end, I gathered my courage and approached Vivienne on the way out the door. "May I speak with you?" I asked. My voice sounded strange. I'd never said a word to her out loud.

She raised an eyebrow. "Come on," she said.

I was shaking as I followed her past Madame Sivenko's office. She led me to a conference room with a large mahogany table surrounded by swivel chairs.

"Have a seat," she said, and I did as instructed. The leather chair was freezing. We looked at each other for a minute while she let her hair out of a bun into a ponytail. I grew cold in my uniform of black leotard, pink tights, and pointe shoes.

She sat and crossed her muscular legs. Her face didn't have a drop of makeup. No student my age would dare leave their dorm room like that, but she looked beautiful.

"I suppose you're here about your conference," she said.

"What can I do to prove myself next year?" I asked.

"Look." She smoothed her chiffon skirt and folded her arms. "You didn't grow. The shortest BNY dancers are at least five foot five, and you're still five foot two."

So, they *were* disappointed in me because I didn't grow enough. I'd never realized that was their expectation, that my body would change more. Why hadn't Madame Sivenko said it?

She squinted as if she were trying to figure me out. "At least you're coming back and promoted a level. Next year, get yourself in the race, at least for the exposure to companies beyond BNY. You usually stand in the back and let the more confident students push in front of you. This is not a place to put others first."

Her words shook me up. Was *that* how she perceived me? "I know why I'm here," I said, determined.

"It's not easy to hear, but dancers are disposable," she said, not unkindly. "We don't cater to hopes and dreams. Most people can't get a job. The ones who do make it into a company, even a small one, rarely make it out of the corps. Is that what you want?"

"It doesn't matter where I get a job," I lied, biting my fingernail. "I just want to dance." The minute I said the words, they sounded like such a cliché.

She was having none of my sucking up. "Let's be honest. You care. If you didn't, you wouldn't have come here. All the dancers in BNY have natural talent and facility. You're setting yourself up for a letdown if you want something you're not suited for."

"Are you saying I'm not going to make it?" I asked, feeling foolish that she'd been my favorite teacher all year. The notion that she was on my side was fading fast.

"I know you love it," she said. "I watch dancers every day. I can see everything by how you dance."

"I love it more than anything."

She leaned forward, placed her elbows on her knees, and looked me in the eye. "Anna," she said. "You like dancing because it comes naturally to you. You have beautiful feet, good proportions, and nice extensions, but unless a miracle happens, at five foot two, you'll probably be too short for BNY. Maybe you need to dance, but I don't think you understand what it means to become a professional."

She leaned back in her chair.

We looked at each other. I opened my mouth and then shut it again, unsure why I was there at all. How could I escape a dream I'd had almost my entire life? I was angry at myself for wanting this so much.

"I can't predict the future," she said. "We'll have to see what next year brings."

I stood and wiped away the tears running down my face. "Thank you for talking to me. Next year will be different."

"Good." She swiveled her chair back and forth, looking thoughtful. "Come back ready to work."

CHAPTER 7

I flew home to Rock Island for a week in June. Mom left a stack of newspaper clippings on my desk: articles about the Rock Island Ballet in the local paper, Ballet New York articles in The *New York Times*, articles about the importance of breast exams, osteoporosis prevention, and dealing with competition.

I helped set the dinner table, remembering all the good meals I'd eaten on these dishes. "I wanted to make this visit good for you," Mom said. "Who knows how much longer you'll keep coming back?" She couldn't stop hugging me.

We sat down to eat when Dad came home from cycling class. "Since when do you go to the gym?" I asked.

"Since our house turned into an empty nest," he said.

Mom added, "I started yoga."

They looked healthy and happier than they had before I left. I'd missed important events in their lives while I'd been gone. On the surface it was like nothing had changed at home, but I could sense the ground shifting beneath me.

Dad bit into a chicken leg. "Great dinner, Sue. Anna should come home more often. You haven't cooked a meal this good in ages."

Mom smacked his shoulder.

I said, "Don't get used to it. I'm off to San Francisco soon."

"We know," Mom said, and I heard the catch in her throat.

It was hard being away.

As much as I loved them, the more times I went away and came back, the more I felt like a guest in my old home.

I flew into San Francisco on a Saturday morning. During the flight, I played Stravinsky on my headphones and imagined myself nailing six *pirouettes* in the middle of a performance of *Fire*. I was so caught up in my dancing fantasy that I almost missed my luggage on the carousel.

The fog-covered hills and pastel houses were a new world to take in on the taxi ride into San Francisco. What a change from the skyscrapers and pedestrians in Manhattan. I loved how different it was from anywhere I'd been, and looked for some sign, any sign, of where I belonged. Which place was *me*? I wondered if Charles Diamond, the artistic director, would be around during the summer session.

Our sublet was in a complex on a busy street, and as we pulled up, I looked at the windows and pictured Jen and Marie inside, going about their lives.

The driver opened the door to help me out of the cab. I climbed out and paid him, insisting I didn't need help with my bags. I'd dragged more luggage in New York, after all. He watched with a concerned expression as I lugged my duffel toward the door.

The elevator took me up to the eighth floor. I walked down the hall toward our condo and knocked, excited to see my friends.

"You're here," Jen said, throwing the door open. She was in jeans and a T-shirt and looked happier than the last time I saw her. We hugged each other tight.

"I missed you," I said. It felt more like coming home to family than my trip to Rock Island. Marie appeared behind Jen, smiling in her reserved way. I was so happy I never had to live with Hilary again.

"We've been waiting for you," Marie said. Her blond hair was down, her face was makeup-free for the first time, and I was shocked to see her wearing jeans, too.

I followed them into the apartment, which was small but nicely furnished with a view of the street. We decided easily that Jen and I would share the large bedroom with two singles, and Marie took the smaller room with the double bed. After unpacking, I went to the living room and jumped on the sofa.

I leaped from the couch to the sofa chair as Jen walked out of our bedroom. It seemed so long ago that I was nervous about attending the SBNY summer course. Now, six weeks seems like an eternity to *be* at home.

"We're going to be tourists on the weekends," Jen said, watching me bounce off the furniture like a little kid. "I refuse to spend the whole summer in the studio."

Marie joined us, and I flopped down on the floor and said, "We're seventeen and on our own in San Francisco. We shouldn't spend all our time staring in the mirror."

But staring in the mirror was precisely what I intended to do. I pointed my foot in front of me and examined the high arch, fantasizing about how much I'd improve in this new environment.

Jen and I could say we wanted to act like regular teenagers, but one of the reasons we got along so well was that we knew deep down that ballet was the priority.

Jen placed in the top class in San Francisco, one level above Marie and me, just like it was at SBNY. We didn't see the dorm kids much outside of class, so we spent our free time together, and did get out on the weekends to explore the tourist spots like Fisherman's Wharf, Ghirardelli

Square, Golden Gate Park, Haight Street, Chinatown, and North Beach.

Marie and Jen hadn't known each other as well I knew them in New York, but after eating every meal together, walking to and from ballet, hanging out at the apartment, and exploring the city together, the SBNY dynamic faded into the past. By the second week, we could read each other's thoughts. I'd never had closer friends.

On the second Saturday, after wandering through Golden Gate Park, we went out for dinner. Marie marched past the line to get our names in for a table. We were seeing a new side of her in San Francisco. She was more uninhibited than she'd ever been in New York.

Jen grabbed my arm and said, "Is Marie flirting with the manager so we can cut the line?"

A minute later, Marie gestured at us to follow her to a booth by the window. The manager who gave us our menus looked like a college student.

"This was so nice of you," Marie said, and she touched his arm. The look on his face made me laugh. He knew what she was doing and didn't seem to mind.

"Let me know if you need anything," he said. "I'll be sure to send over some dessert." He winked at us before he walked away.

"Jamal, who?" Jen asked.

A blush crept up Marie's neck. Jen said the manager was cute. I unfolded my napkin and looked down at my plate.

"It's about time for you to have a love interest," Marie told Jen.

"I want to know where you're getting this new confidence," I said, thinking of how Marie liked Jamal all year, and nothing came of it the same way nothing happened between Tyler and me. "How many of us had crushes in New York and never had the nerve to act on them?"

Marie said, "The people here can't make or break my future. Our San Francisco teachers and any boys we meet now will come and go. Doesn't it feel different to you?"

"No," Jen said. "I feel the same."

"I see your point," I said. "Give me a dare."

"Well, well, well," Marie said.

"Anna," Jen said, "Please don't make me regret going out in public with you."

Marie leaned over and whispered to me. I nodded, enjoying Jen's anxious expression.

After a minute, I nodded at Marie and winked.

Jen said, "What are you up to?"

"Oh, nothing, just eat," Marie said as the food arrived. We fell silent as Jen ate her Caesar salad one small bite at a time. Marie politely nibbled her veggie burger, and I devoured my chicken sandwich. When I'd finished, I dug a pen out of my purse, grabbed a napkin, and stood up.

"I'll be right back," I said.

"Where are you going?" Jen asked.

I walked over to the table next to us. The two middle-aged couples look friendly.

"Excuse me," I said, "my friend and I—the blonde—are taking a short survey. Should our other friend there ask the manager on a date?" I pointed at Jen.

They looked at me, bewildered for a minute, and then the burly-looking guy with a beard said, "You're only young once."

"Right on," said the woman with him. She gave me a thumbs up.

"So that's a 'yes?'" I confirmed.

"Yes," they said in agreement.

"Thanks," I said and moved on to the following table.

Marie was laughing hysterically. Jen covered her face with her hands. The next group had three women, and at first, they voted no. Once I walked away, they called me back to change their answer. The table after that was all guys, and they said yes before I even asked the question.

Jen was mortified when I returned to the table. "I can't believe you," she said.

"What's the big deal?" I asked. "Everyone in this restaurant thinks you should follow your heart."

"I knew it," Marie said. "We've all been holding ourselves back out of fear."

"There's no way," Jen said, looking visibly upset, enough that I second-guessed myself and felt bad for embarrassing her. Marie went to find our server to pay, and I followed Jen outside, thanking the other tables a second time on my way out.

Jen had tears in her eyes. I hugged her and apologized; she said sorry, too, and tried to shake it off. Marie joined us, and we started down the hill.

"Hey, wait up," a voice called from behind. To my surprise, the cute manager was running toward us. We stopped and waited for him.

"Excuse me," he said, catching his breath. "This is sort of awkward, but I was wondering if I could have your phone number."

"Well—" Marie began.

"No," he interrupted, "you." He looked right at Jen.

"Me?" Jen said in a dumbfounded way.

I laughed so hard at the shocked look on Jen's face.

"You're stunning," he said to her, and he was right and meant it sincerely. Jen turned bright red.

"I'm sorry," she finally managed, "but I'm only seventeen, and you seem . . ."

"Oh," he said, surprised. "I thought you were much older."

She smiled. "I'm not."

He nodded in an embarrassed way. "Okay, got it. Bye."

We watched him leave before we looked at each other in disbelief. Nothing remotely like that had happened to any of us before.

To my disappointment, Charles Diamond looked in on my class only once for five minutes the entire summer. He had danced with BNY a generation ahead of Victor and had a kind face.

On the bright side, my technique and self-confidence improved. Most weekdays were routine: technique class at ten, lunch with Jen and Marie at noon, *pointe* class at two, and either jazz, character, modern, or *pas de deux* at four.

Halfway through the summer, a teacher got sick, and the school combined the two upper levels that day. It was my first time in a class with Jen and a preview of what it would be like for all three of us to be together at SBNY.

Jen and Marie stood together at one of the portable barres. I chose an empty place along the back wall. Competing with friends made me so uncomfortable.

I put my right leg up on the barre to stretch. My body was in good shape after six weeks of intensive classes with no school in the way.

A tall man in running pants and a white T-shirt entered the studio. I assumed he was our guest teacher from the company, Alejandro Lopez. "Let's begin," he said, clapping his hands.

He'd taught Jen's class before, but not mine. She had said he was from Caracas and came to San Francisco as a student when he was fifteen. He'd had classical training, and his manner and movements were much more formal than the energetic Roizman style.

"He's gorgeous," the girl beside me whispered, stating the obvious.

Alejandro strolled around the room to inspect us during the first combination. The atmosphere at the San Francisco school was different than at SBNY; it wasn't any less strict, but the classes felt slower-paced and friendlier.

During the *plié* combination, Alejandro stopped to adjust Jen's arm. He lifted her chin up a fraction of an inch. She glowed under the attention, and Marie watched out of the corner of her eye and stood straighter.

We progressed through the usual series of footwork. I focused on the corrections I'd heard over and over lately from different teachers: to keep my shoulders down and use my abdominal muscles to stop swaying my back.

Sweat and makeup dripped into my eyes by the time we started the *fondus.*

Forty-five minutes later, Alejandro signaled for us to clear the portable barres. We came to the center of the room. Dancers took a minute to stretch, put on their pointe shoes, or grab a drink of water. At the San Francisco school, pointe shoes were optional at the barre, but of course, Jen, Marie, and I all had our pointe shoes on already. After a year at SBNY, I couldn't imagine dancing in technique shoes, not even at the barre.

Alejandro demonstrated the first center combination, pointing his feet to the front, back, and side and finishing with a turn. I marked the combination with my hands to memorize the sequence. Dancers slowly trickled back in and found their own space in the room.

"Let's go. The first group," Alejandro said. He was stern, with no smile. Jen and Marie stood right in front of the mirror, and most of the dancers from the higher class stepped forward.

Vivienne's voice came into my mind, telling me to have courage and go to the front. But watching how easily Jen and Marie marched up there made me want to do the opposite. Jen had been at the top of her class in New York, but she pulled ahead of the pack even more in San Francisco. She was the best. How could Victor have passed her over?

I wasn't wired to push myself to the front, but Vivienne's voice told me to go forward.

Come on, I told myself. *Do you want this or not?* I forced myself to stand front and center when Alejandro called for the second group.

Jen and Marie watched me from the side of the room, and the combination went fine. But when the music ended, Alejandro crossed his arms and stood before me. He smelled like expensive cologne and was even better looking up close.

I held the last pose, looking directly over my fingers to finish the line of my body just as Madame Sivenko had taught me. Knowing she'd trained me gave me confidence.

"You're an SBNY student," he said, recognizing the signature style of a Roizman *pirouette*, the longer line in the preparation and finish. I waited for him to correct me, but he didn't, so I dropped the pose and straightened up to stare at him.

"I can't stand that way of turning," he said.

My jaw dropped. Jen and I made eye contact in the mirror.

"You think that *pirouette* looked nice," he continued, "but you have no solid foundation for your turn without both legs in *plié* at the beginning. Show me a real *pirouette*."

Shaken, I bent my back knee and executed the *pirouette* again, flawlessly, the way dancers did it before Roizman influenced classical ballet. I longed for my teachers in New

York, especially Vivienne and Matthew. It felt strange to do a turn the way I used to in Rock Island.

Alejandro nodded, "See? Better."

I smiled sweetly at him, knowing I'd return to doing it the Roizman way when I went to my next class.

During the last combination, I waltzed and leaped with five other girls in a circle around the room. In the mirror, my cheeks looked bright red. Letting my body fly when every muscle was thoroughly warmed up felt great.

Jen was stretching her calves on the tilted calf board when I finished. A third group of girls formed a circle in the middle of the room to repeat the exercise.

"Hey," Jen whispered. "I watched you today. You're pretty good."

She had never commented on my ability, and I was taken aback.

I jumped to the defensive. "You don't have to sound so surprised."

"No, that's not what I meant," Jen said, and I realized she was looking at me with new respect. "I just never saw you dance before."

It dawned on me how odd it was that we'd been friends for so long and talked about so many ballet-related issues without her knowing what kind of dancer I was or if I was any good. I said, "Thanks."

"Class dismissed," Alejandro said, and the room broke out in scattered applause. Jen, Marie, and I gathered our bags and headed toward the door together. As everyone exited the room, I had a sense of dèja-vu. One class faded into the next.

We went to Union Square on our last weekend, and after a few hours of shopping, we took a cable car to Fisherman's Wharf. The area was crowded and humming with tourists. Jen was camera-happy and walked in front of us, taking action shots.

"Cut it out," Marie said, charging ahead into the Ghirardelli chocolate store. We followed her. There were enormous barrels of chocolate, and we wandered through, tasting samples and picking out presents. I wanted the day to go on forever.

After I paid, I walked outside to find my friends. They were sitting on a bench next to the pier. I sat down next to Marie.

She was in the middle of a thought. "I've been reconsidering what I want."

Jen said, "Don't be silly. Your drive will return once you're back in New York. You left your family in Paris for this."

What had they been talking about? "You don't want to be a dancer anymore, Marie? What else would you do?"

"It's probably a phase," Marie said, but she looked troubled. "This summer has been so nice. I don't want to go back to all the competition and craziness. Why can't we have fun, eat whatever we want, and not worry so much?" She stood and walked toward the railing.

Jen and I looked at each other. The mood had suddenly turned so heavy.

"I can't imagine switching direction after everything we've already been through," Jen said. The wind blew her hair in her face, but I could see the anxiety there.

"I almost quit once," I said, "When I was thirteen. My mom and my ballet teacher talked me out of it. I wanted to focus on horseback riding, which was stupid because we couldn't afford it anyway. At the time, my parents didn't realize how expensive the pointe shoes would become."

Jen watched Marie lean on the rail and look into the water. "I'd never quit now," Jen said.

I wondered what would happen if Jen didn't get a job. Had she forgotten that Victor said her shoulders were too broad and her chest was too big? The whole thing was garbage. She was a gorgeous dancer, but after those comments, if I were her, I'd be worried.

"What if I joined the circus?" asked Marie when she returned.

We stood, quiet for a moment, just thinking. Marie crossed her arms.

"Your sweater," I said, pointing. The sleeves of her expensive black cardigan were covered in goop that must have been on the rail where she'd rested her arms.

She looked at her elbows and shrieked.

"I think that stuff keeps the birds away," Jen said, eyes wide.

None of us said it, but the ruined sweater felt like an omen.

CHAPTER 8

After two weeks of hanging out with my parents and Rachel in Rock Island, I returned to New York, ready to take on my senior year. The end of August in the city was hot and humid, but I was so happy to be back.

During my first class as an upper division student, Simon indicated a small jump combination when the door opened unexpectedly. Bruce Pollock, the instantly recognizable director of National Ballet Theatre, walked into the studio. He was a tall, bald man with spectacles. NBT was the leading classical ballet troupe in the United States, and the other major company in New York besides BNY.

Simon stopped demonstrating to shake Bruce's hand. They whispered while we stood waiting, nervous and excited.

"What's he doing here?" I asked Marie. We huddled together in the back of the studio.

She went up and down on pointe, looking nervous. "No idea," she whispered back.

The discussion at the front of the room dragged on. I tried to lip read Simon and Bruce's words but failed. They seemed to be looking at Jen. I studied myself in the mirror and decided it was a skinny day. NBT dancers weren't as tall as those at BNY, so maybe Bruce would like me.

At last, Simon gestured to us to start the *petit allegro*. He nodded at the pianist. Bruce took a seat at the front of the room.

The rest of the class felt like an audition. Jen had the most seniority, so we deferred to her to take the lead. Nicole and Hilary pushed up front beside her and repeated every combination.

I should have made myself seen, but instead, I hid behind Marie in the second group. She was off her competitive game, too. It almost seemed like she didn't care.

We finished the *grand révérence* at the end, and everyone clapped. We were dripping with sweat. Bruce walked over to whisper to Simon.

"Will Jen please stay after for a moment," Simon announced.

My heart pounded so hard that my chest felt like it might explode. There was a half-second of hesitation, and then we all went about our business as if nothing unusual had happened.

Jen approached the front of the room, and she seemed calm, even though I was sure she was coming out of her skin. I left to wait for her in the hall.

NBT had an opening they needed to fill fast. That was the only reason Bruce Pollock would have come. Why was I emotional over something I didn't even know I wanted? Jen was the best dancer in the school. Of course, he'd pick her. But what was wrong with me?

Jen walked out of the studio after a few minutes, smiling. She came over and whispered, "He invited me to take company class with NBT tomorrow."

I stared wide-eyed at her as she squeezed my hand.

"Congratulations," I said. My face felt hot.

She said, "This is nuts. Today felt like any other day. I've got to call my parents." She dropped my hand and hurried down the hall.

I watched her go, amazed at how quickly it happened.

The following day, Jen woke up before me, which threw off my usual routine. Most mornings, she was the one who slept late.

"*Merde*," I said, which dancers always say for good luck. When she was ready, I stopped doing my hair to hug her, but she only stood there, pale and trembling. She left for the NBT studios downtown before I went to school.

I thought about Jen all day as I sat through Algebra and French, took morning technique class, ate lunch, and returned to YAH for American History. By pointe class, I was desperate to know what had happened. If NBT hired her, we'd celebrate that moment we all dreamed of. She could tell her family and her local ballet school that she'd made it and that the investment and sacrifice had been worth it.

I was counting on her to prove that the struggle paid off.

When I reached our room, Jen sat on our windowsill and stared at the plaza. Her profile was beautiful. Determination emanated from her. She turned her head and looked at me.

"Well?" I asked.

"They offered me an apprenticeship."

"Oh my God!" I shouted.

"Everyone at home is going to freak out," she said. "I'll get to dance *La Bayadère* and *Giselle* and *Romeo and Juliet*. The classical ballets I'd never perform at BNY."

I sat across from her. "You're taking it, I assume?"

She bit her lip. I felt the weight of her dilemma. If she accepted, she'd shut the door to BNY. Switching from NBT to BNY was like moving from the Mets to the Yankees.

"Madame Sivenko told me to take the job." Her voice sounded sad.

I could only imagine how much that hurt for her to hear. She was the best female dancer in the school but was also the only one left from last year's upper-level class. Everyone else had quit or received a job.

Her eyes looked exhausted. "Victor said I don't have the right aesthetic line."

"But you're a stick." She hardly ate, only cereal and vegetables.

"I know what you're thinking," she said.

"I was thinking how hard you've worked and what an accomplishment this is." I looked out the window, but she stared at me until I met her gaze.

"I'll never be good enough for them," she said. Her tone was flat.

I tried to snap her out of it. "NBT is a fantastic company."

"Oh, stop," she said. "I'm a failure."

"A failure?" It was so sad. She'd been handed this incredible opportunity, and all she could think about was how she didn't get into Ballet New York.

"I've been planning to join BNY since I was a little girl," she said. "Ask my mom. If my ballet teachers told me to do something, I did it. My brothers played soccer and had friends, but I had ballet. My mom took me on a New York trip every spring since I was nine to see BNY perform. My family gave money to the school and the company. Since I moved here for my sophomore year, I've had regular conferences with Madame Sivenko about what I had to do to get in. I've tried more diets than I can count. What did I do wrong?"

I wasn't ready for her to share the extent of her desperation. It didn't surprise me, but we never discussed it. Don't ask, and don't tell.

I didn't want to know.

"You just got into one of the top ballet companies in the world," I said, understanding but also wanting to smack her. "We should be celebrating."

"It doesn't mean anything," she said. She put her face in her hands.

"Maybe you should talk to someone about this," I said.

"I'm talking to you," she said. "Who else would I talk to? People outside this world would never understand."

CHAPTER 9

Jen's departure left a void in the upper-level class. I missed having her to look up to, but her absence pushed me to grow. It was one thing to stay in the back when Jen was in the front, but I didn't want Hilary and Nicole to be the class stars once she'd gone. So I forced myself to dance in the first group and the front line. The more I put myself forward, the more I believed I belonged there.

As the weeks passed, my approach changed. I thought more deeply about my movements. Dancing became a craft. I envisioned how I wanted a step to look, and more and more, I could turn that vision into reality. I'd reached a new level of awareness. For so long, I had struggled to translate the ideal into my body, and suddenly, after almost fifteen years of training, I could do it.

In November, Victor taught our class. It was the first time he would see most of us dance, and the pressure brought out our best and worst.

"Why so tense?" Hilary asked me when I walked into the studio, still out of breath from the rush to return from

YAH. She had on a new low-cut velvet leotard. "Is it because of the rumor that Victor is already deciding on apprenticeships for next spring?"

I ignored her and went to my barre spot.

Hilary moved on to someone else and said, "Faye, do you think you should wear those legwarmers? I'd wear mine, but I don't want him to think I'm hiding cellulite or anything. Is my stomach sticking out today? God, I feel bloated." She turned sideways to look at her reflection and pooched her stomach out.

Faye said, "Hilary, you look fine," and peeled off her legwarmers.

Poor Faye. She was perfectly nice but still lived at home in Queens and remained on the outskirts of the social scene. Her technique had improved over the summer, so Hilary and Nicole had decided she was more of a threat, but Faye still seemed to save her energy rather than use it. Her dancing always looked like she was holding something back.

Nicole was dealing with her nerves differently. "Why is my face breaking out?" Nicole said, spritzing her dark hair with hairspray and annoying the girls beside her. They looked relieved when she walked to the mirror to apply lip gloss.

"Can Hilary and Nicole hear themselves?" Marie whispered. We tied the ribbons on our pointe shoes.

Vivienne followed Victor into the room. His teaching outfit was jeans, a T-shirt, and sneakers. Even Vivienne looked tense. She was so tiny next to him that she barely reached his chest.

Victor looked like the kind of person who thought he knew everything.

There was something cold about how he leaned on the piano, scanning the room for several minutes before he clapped his hands to begin. Vivienne took a seat in front to observe. Her eyes traveled from one of us to the next.

During the barre, Victor focused only on Nicole. He spent a full five minutes analyzing her *tendu*. It was all I could do not to scream, and looking around the room, I saw every other girl going crazy, too. Only Nicole was happy. The rest of us were heartbroken.

His combinations were simple, designed so he could only observe, not necessarily to teach. His eyes seemed to look everywhere at once. I couldn't read his expression. I wanted to be what he was looking for—whatever that was—but I didn't know how. Any confidence I'd started with drained away as the minutes ticked by. I fell back into my old habit of hiding.

Incredibly, for once, wishing was enough.

"You," Victor said, pointing at me in the back corner as I finished a jump combination. "Come here and demonstrate."

Surprised, I walked forward to the center of the room. "Dancers, watch," he commanded.

My classmates surrounded me, some checking my image in the mirror and some staring directly. I stepped into fifth position to repeat the combination, aware of Vivienne's piercing eyes. At that moment, I cared most about pleasing her. I wanted to make her proud.

Victor gestured to the pianist to play an introduction: *Five, six, seven, eight* . . . I launched myself into the air. *Sissone, assemblé. Sissone, assemblé.* I silently said the steps in my head while I danced them. *Sous-sous, entrechat six. Sous-sous, entrechat six.*

Entrechat six—when we jumped and switched our fifth position foot back, front, back in the air—was one of the most challenging steps in our vocabulary, and it was my specialty. I was the only dancer in the class who could execute *entrechat six* cleanly, every time, and hit all the beats. Most of the other dancers muddled through the step or faked it.

"Good," Victor said in his booming voice. The class clapped politely. He continued, "Notice her musicality. Roizman ballets are visual representations of the music. The sound creates the impetus in your body. You should anticipate what's next without cheating the music. This girl has an innate willingness to be in the moment. Beautiful."

The class nodded, swallowing their jealousy. I bit my lip to keep from grinning.

Hilary practiced *sous-sous, entrechat six* in front of Victor.

"I need to *see* the music," he said, pointing at Hilary's feet. "Don't forget to take a deeper *plié* before the *entrechat six*." He gestured to me. "She's the only one giving me the complete six beats."

Vivienne had a look of pride on her face when she caught my eye. It was the best moment.

I allowed myself to hope. Maybe I'd distinguished myself in front of Victor enough that my height wouldn't matter.

After class ended, I collapsed on the floor in the hallway. My body ached, I was sore in muscles I didn't know I had, and I tingled all over, but I had never felt happier.

I sat up to untie my pointe shoes. One of the younger students approached me. Her face was familiar because she looked in on the advanced class whenever our door was open. I'd often seen her mom, an intense ballet mother, in the lobby.

"You're my favorite dancer in the school," the girl said. Her dark hair was pulled back so tight.

"Thanks," I said. She reminded me of my thirteen-year-old reflection. I saw the same obsession in her eyes.

"I'd give anything to have your feet," she said.

I smiled. "Let me see yours."

She pointed her foot. Her arch was high in her instep, a beautiful bow-shape.

I teased, "I'll trade you."

Her grin was the best. "How do you always look so happy when you dance?" she asked.

She'd caught me off-guard. All I could do was stare at her, surprised at how little I knew myself.

She waved goodbye and skipped off to class.

"Hey, Forester." Tyler passed me on his way to the studio. A distance between us had formed over the summer, and we hadn't hung out much this year. "I heard you impressed the boss today." He leaned over and squeezed my shoulder, which snapped me out of the daze. I looked up at him. He winked at me, which made my heart leap inside my chest. His upper body was solid muscle; he'd grown several inches over the summer.

I walked down the hall toward the water fountain. Before I rounded the corner, I stooped to pull up my leg warmers. Nicole's voice floated around the corner. "I can't believe Victor had her demonstrate."

"She's not even good," Hilary said.

Nicole snickered. "Now, Hilary, let's be nice."

"I wouldn't be smiling if I were that short," Hilary said. "I'd be filling out my college applications."

I hesitated, filling up with familiar anger. They walked around the corner.

"Were you talking about me?" I asked, startling them.

Hilary blinked. "Why would we be talking about you?" she said innocently.

Nicole averted her eyes. They walked right past me without another word.

Their negativity and competitiveness sucked all the joy out of ballet. I kicked my foot into the wall so hard I screamed.

SBNY agreed to let Jen remain in the dorm throughout the school year despite her apprenticeship with NBT. At first, I was glad I didn't have to deal with a new roommate, but as time passed, I felt left behind whenever she talked about her new experiences. We were still close, but we rarely had time to hang out. The circumstances pushed us apart.

I spent many evenings alone in our room, playing music and appreciating the quiet time. On the nights Jen didn't perform, she sewed shoes and fell asleep early, exhausted, while I sat at my desk, conjugating French verbs or writing English papers.

After a fast Rock Island trip for the Thanksgiving holiday, Jen and I hung Christmas lights in our room. Things had been good. Victor noticed me, Vivienne constantly corrected me, Hilary and Nicole treated me like genuine competition, and the school in New Jersey hired me for *Nutcracker*.

A professional career felt increasingly within reach. SBNY wasn't as overwhelming anymore.

The phone rang. I was standing on my desk, thumb-tacking a row of lights across the ceiling.

"It's for you," Jen said, handing me the phone.

"That's weird." My parents were the only ones who called me; I'd just talked to them. I jumped off the desk. "Hello?"

"It's Tyler."

My mouth went dry. He'd never called me before. Last year, he always used to drop in, but that hadn't happened this year.

"What's up?" I asked.

"I'm down in the lobby," he said. "I forgot my ID card, and the new security guy won't let me in."

"I'll come down and get you," I said. "It's almost curfew."

"Thanks," he said and hung up.

Jen gave me a funny look. "He likes you," she said.

My heart sped up. "We're just friends."

She smirked and went back to studying her upcoming tour schedule.

I checked my jeans and cream sweater in the mirror. I liked the prospect of seeing Tyler after ballet hours, in my street clothes and with my hair down. That was rare this year.

I rode the elevator downstairs. The door opened. There he was, stretched out across a bench in the lobby, wearing a dress shirt and jeans. His eyes were closed. I pushed through the turnstile, walked over, and sat at his feet. He smelled different, like cologne—something musky that seemed too grown up for him.

"Hey, sleepy," I said, nudging him. "Curfew in five."

"Thanks for coming," he said with his eyes closed.

"Where have you been?" I asked, and he was quiet long enough to intimidate me. How did things get awkward between us?

"I had a date," he said.

I paused for a moment. "With?"

"Bergitte Pedersen."

I couldn't believe it. "The new Danish girl in the corps?"

"The drop-dead gorgeous one," he said. He sat up and ran a hand through his hair. His eyes sparkled.

I stood up and put my hands on my hips. "You're such a liar."

"She's been flirting with me at company parties."

"Since when do you go to company parties?"

"I have friends in high places," he said, standing up, his body uncomfortably close to mine. "Come here." He took my hand and pulled me to stand beside him, enough that our faces almost touched.

Who was this cocky kid? He was someone I didn't recognize.

I pushed him away and said, "Well, good for you." No way was I missing curfew for this. I showed the security guard my ID and explained that Tyler had left his upstairs. The guard nodded and let Tyler through the gate while I beeped through the turnstile.

He followed me into the elevator.

"Do you like her?" I asked him when the doors closed. He didn't make eye contact. His eyes fixed on the numbers, and I couldn't read him. The elevator door dinged and opened on his floor.

"Do you like her?" I asked again.

He shrugged. "I don't know," he said. He glanced back at me as he walked out of the elevator, but the doors closed before I could figure out how to respond.

On a Thursday night in December, Marie and I went out after we finished our homework. We browsed at the bookstore for an hour, then walked back across the plaza toward the dorms. Charlie and Nicole were standing by the front door. We could see them from far away.

White flakes stuck to our hair and eyelashes, the year's first real snow. Charlie and Nicole were the kids who smoked cigarettes. They didn't care about the rules. Nicole once explained that smoking was a bonding exercise. She said the ritual comforted her. Later, Hilary said that some company dancers used cigarettes to suppress their appetite, and that's why Nicole did it.

"Didn't their parents teach them how bad cigarettes are for their health? Don't they have a tougher time breathing when they dance?" I asked Marie.

She didn't know. "They get by, I guess."

"What's a little lung cancer down the road?" I joked, but it wasn't funny.

"No one wants to think about the future," Marie said. "It's too hard to imagine."

As we approached, I realized Charlie and Nicole weren't alone. Three boys were leaning against the railing next to each other. "Since when are Tyler, Jesse, and Jamal part of that crowd?" I asked.

What shocked me was Tyler holding a cigarette and blowing gray plumes of smoke up into the air. Hilary, Nicole, Jamal, and Charlie huddled in a small half-circle a few feet away. Tyler saw my expression and gave me a warning look that meant "Don't be a goody-two-shoes."

I swallowed how upset I was to see him smoking.

We reached them, and Marie went to talk to Jamal. He smiled when he saw her coming.

Tyler was telling Jesse a story, and when I stood next to Tyler, he said, "Then he eloped with this gorgeous physical therapist who worked with all the dancers. All the girls in the company were heartbroken."

"William Mason," Jesse explained, catching my eye. "The most famous male dancer in Ballet New York history. Tyler's educating me."

I perked up. "He was a god." I'd read William Mason's autobiography and the two other books written about him.

"Anna's idol is Stacy Hannah," Tyler said as he messed up my hair.

I swatted his hand away and said, "She originated the principal role in *Fire*, my favorite ballet. Stacy Hannah was short, fast, and all personality. Stacy and William were invited to dance at the White House for three presidents." I wanted to be Stacy Hannah.

"What a bunhead," Jesse said in a teasing tone. "You're worse than all the girls back home in Orange County."

"William Mason was the original lead in *Fire*," Tyler said. He took a long drag off his cigarette.

I made a disgusted face and moved away from him. "Since when do you do that, anyway? Ick." I waved the smoke out of my face and continued, "William shattered the image that all male ballet dancers are gay. He was such a masculine guy."

"Of course, they're not all gay," Jesse said. "Look at me."

"Anna has more important things to do," Tyler said rudely.

"Excuse me?" I said, as my irritation with Tyler grew. "Since when do you run my life?"

They laughed, but Tyler's behavior hurt. The more I tried to ignore the disintegration of our friendship, the weirder things felt between us. We rarely even danced together in *pas de deux* class. It dawned on me that he'd acted like he was too good for me since his star turn at last year's Workshop.

We stood in silence and watched the theatergoers walking across the plaza through the snow. I picked up bits of the other conversations: Charlie was telling Nicole and Hilary about a movie he'd seen last weekend, and Jamal was teaching Marie the words to Tupac's *Me Against the World* and laughing at her French accent.

Tyler took a drag off his cigarette. I wondered if he enjoyed making me mad.

"Do you know William Mason's full story?" I asked, trying to smooth over the awkwardness.

Jesse and Tyler looked at me and said nothing.

"Well then, I'll tell you," I continued. "He was born on a horse farm in Montana. His dad wanted him to be a rancher, but he saw the girls attending ballet lessons whenever he ran errands in town. One day, he followed a girl he had a crush on, and the teacher got him to take the class. So of course, he fell in love with the girl and got completely hooked on dance."

"Sounds familiar," Jesse said. He hopped up on the ledge and let his legs swing back and forth. Tyler leaned against the wall next to him. I admired them: rugged Jesse and charming Tyler. They made a good-looking pair.

"William's father didn't find out for two years that he was taking ballet," I continued. "One day, he happened to be in town and saw William coming out of dance class with his ballet shoes in hand. He beat him within an inch of his life. William had one more year left of high school but ran away from home. His girlfriend was obsessed with Ballet New York, so he had it in his head that was the place he'd go. He hitchhiked to New York, slept in Central Park, bagged groceries, and eventually, SBNY took him. A few months later, Roizman stopped by the school, saw him flying around the room, and invited him to join the company."

"And then," Tyler chimed in, "He had a twenty-five-year career of standing ovations, honors, awards, TV, over thirty Roizman ballets including *Fire* choreographed for him, and covers of *Dance, Time, Newsweek, Vanity Fair*—the works."

"Plus, he had affairs with practically every girl in the company," I added.

Jesse said, "And now he's the Los Angeles Ballet Theater director."

"One of the top companies in the country," said Tyler.

"But he's not Victor Caldwell," I said.

"I'd take William Mason any day over Victor Caldwell," Tyler said. "Victor was nowhere near as exciting a dancer, and he's kind of a jerk from what I hear."

We were quiet again, pondering all the history that preceded us. Jesse stood and stretched his arms over his head. He yawned before crossing his arms and leaning back against the ledge next to Tyler. It grew colder outside.

Hilary walked over to Jesse and put her arms around his shoulders. She whispered in his ear, but Jesse wasn't having it with her. Tyler and I exchanged a glance.

Jesse stepped around Hilary and came toward me. "I've been thinking I should try dancing with you in partnering class," he said.

"Me?" I asked, taken by surprise. Jesse picked me up by the waist and spun me around.

"Put me down," I said, aware of Tyler and Hilary watching.

"But you're so light," Jesse said. He lifted me higher over his head, looking up into my eyes. The more I struggled, the more it amused him. Finally, he lowered me to the ground, letting my body slide against his.

"What the heck, Jesse," Tyler said. "Quit bothering her."

"I'm not bothering her," Jesse said, letting go of my waist and taking my hand. "We're having a conversation." He didn't take his eyes off mine.

I'd spent the fall so focused on school and ballet that I realized I hadn't thought about boys in forever. The tension reminded me why I'd pushed them out of my mind. Boys were a huge distraction. The sudden attention from Jesse made my imagination come alive.

I sensed Marie, Jamal, Nicole, and Charlie looking at me. Hilary was glaring. I looked at Tyler, most concerned about his reaction, but he stared at the ground.

"I'm going in," Tyler announced. He ground his cigarette with his shoe and walked toward the building.

"Tyler," I called, pulling away from Jesse.

But Tyler didn't look back. He'd already disappeared inside when I started after him, and I stopped, unsure what to do.

"Are you going in?" Marie asked me, breaking away from the other group.

"It's early," Jamal said, grabbing her hand. A flicker of indecision crossed her face.

I looked past Jamal and saw Charlie and Nicole hugging to keep warm. Hilary was arguing with Jesse.

I made eye contact with Jesse and saw a hurt look in his eyes.

Hilary noticed his focus on me. She stopped talking and placed her hand on his shoulder. He glanced down at her briefly, then looked back at me. She saw it and didn't like it.

When I said nothing, Jesse turned to Hilary and said, "Hey, I was just playing around."

"Let's go," I said, pulling Marie away from Jamal. We walked into the building together.

Marie and I said goodnight and didn't discuss it, but as we stood in the elevator without saying anything, I could tell she felt the strangeness of the evening too. I couldn't get Tyler or Jesse out of my head for hours. I lay in bed and re-lived how they'd listened to me tell the story about William Mason. My waist still tingled where Jesse had picked me up. I thought of a dozen things to say to Tyler that I knew I never would.

After an hour of tossing and turning, I finally calmed my mind and fell asleep the only way I could think of—by envisioning that I was dancing a ballet.

CHAPTER 10

After he announced that he wanted to partner with me, Jesse flirted with me when we saw each other in the dorms, at school, in the cafeteria, and especially in front of Tyler. He acted like we had an inside joke. I tried to ignore the attention, but it only seemed to encourage him, and Tyler pulled further away. The smoking pushed the wedge deeper between us.

The more Tyler ignored me, the more I felt like I needed to talk to him and couldn't. It became difficult to think about ballet or school. When I wasn't thinking about Tyler, I tried to determine if Jesse genuinely liked me or was using me to drive Hilary and Nicole crazy. My mind couldn't focus on day-to-day things. The teachers corrected me, and I barely heard them. The ballet schedule became nothing more than a way to anticipate when I'd see Tyler or Jesse next. I forgot myself.

Simon's class became a refuge. For the first time, I was grateful for his silence. I wanted to be left alone. I was so hung up on boys that I didn't care about improving or impressing my teachers or where my career was going. The irony of it all was that I danced better than ever.

Marie, Jamal, and I went to BNY's opening night gala together. Jamal was growing on me. He held the door for us and listened when Marie told him about her worries. They were kind

BNY danced one of my favorite Roizman ballets, *America*. The music was by Sousa, and the choreography used the whole roster—it was a major spectacle of a ballet. Diana Rampling and Richard Jackson danced the *pas de deux*, and they were bold and energetic.

"Can French dancers move that fast?" I teased Marie as we walked past the fountain on our way home.

Jamal said, "This theater is no Opéra Garnier."

"It doesn't matter," Marie said, growing serious. "I'm not sure I want to do this anymore."

I didn't know what to say. I'd sensed she had that feeling on and off starting in the summer, but she hadn't mentioned it since San Francisco. I wondered why she'd brought it up in front of Jamal.

He put his arm around her shoulder.

"Maybe try not to think about it?" I suggested, uncomfortable under the weight of her comment.

"You don't understand," she snapped. "This isn't fun and games. My parents didn't send me from France to fail."

Jamal looked flustered while I struggled with how to respond. None of us came to New York with a guarantee that ballet would work out.

Up ahead, I noticed Tyler walking into the building with Charlie and Hilary. "Why is he hanging out with them?" I asked, hurt.

Jamal said, "You need to get over it."

"I know." But I couldn't.

When we reached the dorm, they said goodnight to me, and Jamal followed Marie to her room. I could hear him humming the music to *America* as he walked away, making me smile.

I let out a sigh. Jen was performing with NBT, and my room was lonely and dull after the excitement of the ballet. I sat on my bed, all dressed up, wishing I could dissect the performance with Tyler like we used to last year. Working up the nerve to go to find him took twenty minutes.

When I entered his suite, I saw light under his door and heard music inside his room. I lost my nerve and just stood there.

His door opened a crack, startling me, and he stuck his head out. "I thought I heard something," he said. He was still dressed up from the gala and looked handsome, with his tie hanging loosely around his neck. His hair was rumpled.

"What are you doing here?' he asked, opening the door so I could step inside.

"I came to visit you."

He ran a hand through his hair, pondered my answer, and sat at his desk chair.

His room was a mess. I'd never seen his space like that before. Potato chips were all over the floor, and the carpet hadn't been vacuumed. There were clothes everywhere.

I leaned against the doorway, wishing I hadn't come.

After a long silence, he said, "I don't need your judgments, OK?"

An exasperated sound escaped me. "Why are you acting this way?"

"You're not my mother, you know," he said.

"You're the most talented guy I've ever met, and I used to think you were the nicest, too. What happened to the person I used to hang out with?" The words sounded awful as soon as they came out. I wanted to take them back.

"I'm not the guy you think I am," he said.

"I guess not," I said, and it came out harsher than I intended. "Why did I use to think we had so much in common?"

"Don't be upset," he said.

I said goodnight and went back to my room.

I was preoccupied with finals the week before the *Nutcracker* in New Jersey. Having something concrete to focus on, like math, was a relief. My thinking about Tyler was circular; it exhausted me and went nowhere.

"He has problems that have nothing to do with you," Jen advised on one of the rare times we saw each other.

I spent every night at my desk, poring over my books, determined to ace my exams. Jen left on tour to California midway through the week, so I had the room to myself for the last few days before break.

I couldn't sit still by ten o'clock the night before my last final, so I grabbed some change and headed for the vending machines in the lobby. When the elevator opened to take me downstairs, I walked right into Jesse on his way up.

"Sorry," I said. I'd been avoiding him lately.

"What's the rush?" he asked, holding the door open. He looked great in khakis and a white polo shirt.

I said "I need a chocolate fix."

"Me too, now that you mention it," he said, stepping back into the elevator with me. The doors closed.

"Where are you coming from?" I asked.

"Dinner with my grandparents," he said. It was the first time I'd heard anything about his family.

"Do they live here?"

"No," he said, "they're visiting from California. They raised me. They're kind of like my parents." We stood across from each other, leaning against opposite sides of the elevator.

"What happened to your real parents?"

"They died in a car accident when I was little," he said.

"I'm so sorry." I couldn't believe I'd known him for over a year and didn't know about this.

We crossed the lobby toward the vending machines area. I glanced at his profile. He suddenly seemed like someone I didn't know at all.

"Did your grandparents want you to be a dancer?" I asked.

"My parents were both dancers with BNY," he said, and I was even more shocked that I didn't know that, either.

The vending machine space was small, and I had to stand close to him. He smelled like soap. I watched him drop quarters into the machine and press the button.

"My grandparents always expected me to go to SBNY and dance with the company, but the truth is, I wanted to do something different," he said, glancing at me. "I like school." He retrieved his candy from the bottom slot.

I stepped ahead to put my change in the machine, fully conscious that he was right behind me. My stomach fluttered when I turned around to face him.

He leaned forward and kissed me on the lips. His fingers grazed my hair. For a moment, all my worries went away.

I was the one who pulled back. "Why did you do that?" I asked, surprised and pleased.

He shrugged. "Why not?"

I tried to stop myself from smiling but couldn't help it. He smiled, too. Then he pulled me in his arms and kissed me again. It was beautiful but frightening, too. I wasn't used to feeling out of control and pushed him away.

"We should go back upstairs," I said, breathless.

"Why?" he asked. "Are you afraid of me?"

I was afraid of how vulnerable I felt, not of him.

"You are trouble," I answered.

We walked back into the elevator. He reached for me again, but I moved away. "That's enough."

"I don't get it," he said with a hurt look. "Is this because you like Tyler?"

How could I explain how nervous I felt around him, and that feeling cared for made me wild with insecurity? What if he decided he liked a different girl next week?

I rushed down the hall toward my room when the elevator doors opened. He followed and grabbed my wrist. I glanced around, anxious someone would see and gossip about us.

"I'm not going to keep chasing you," he said. "But you're giving me mixed signals. Come to my room for a while. We can talk. Nothing else, I promise."

"I'm sorry, I can't," I said, even though I wanted to follow him more than anything. "I'm not ready for this. I need to think."

"You're worried that people will gossip," he said.

"I'm worried I'll lose my focus," I said. "The next few months will make or break my life."

He nodded. "I understand. I do. But you don't have to be so perfect all the time. It's okay to let someone in, someone who cares."

I backed down the hall, turning away from him when I reached the turn toward my suite. When I entered my room, I shut the door and leaned against it, slowly sliding down to a sitting position.

When I brought my hands to my cheeks, they were warm.

Jesse kept his distance during the last week before winter break, even when we all went to New Jersey for *Nutcracker* performances. Marie and I shared a hotel room, and I ate all my meals with her and Jamal. My roles were Doll, Snow, and Marzipan, and I was so excited to perform for the first time in a year and a half. I hadn't been onstage since I'd lived in Rock Island.

I spent an hour before the shows pulling my wet hair into a perfect tight bun, applying base, eyeshadow, eyeliner, false eyelashes, blush, and lipstick. I loved the patchwork satin

Doll dress, the silver Snow costume, and the yellow tutu with pink flowers I wore for Marzipan. Everyone looked so beautiful, all dressed up in full makeup.

The lights added a larger-than-life feeling to the stage, and standing in the wings, I was overwhelmed with pride to be part of something that brought beauty and happiness into people's lives.

Going home for winter break was a relief. When Mom and Dad picked me up from the airport, I couldn't believe how happy I was to see them.

The feeling faded fast.

"We're considering selling the house," Dad said. His face looked drawn and tired, and he forgot to put on his blinker and do a head check before switching lanes. The guy he cut off honked at us.

"We hoped we could keep it until Dad retired," Mom said. "But it makes sense to sell it while the market's good. We don't know what your situation will be next year."

They made so many sacrifices so I could go to SBNY.

"You won't have to worry about paying for college," I said. "I'll have a full-time ballet job next year."

"Maybe, maybe not," Dad said. "You're applying, and we still want you to go to college, whether next year or a few years from now." They'd been discussing my future.

"I don't think you get it," I said. "Ballet is a *career*. I'm not going to college." I looked out the window at the cozy houses and tree-lined streets and couldn't imagine returning to this kind of life.

"We know, we know," Dad said. "We're just saying you might feel differently about it when you're twenty-five."

"No. I won't."

Mom said, "Let's just drop it for now."

We rode the rest of the way in silence.

During my week at home, they said nothing further about college or the house, but I could sense the future wearing on them.

It was wearing on me, too.

Rachel picked me up the night before Christmas. We went to the McDonald's drive-thru and ordered French fries, soda, and ice cream cones. While we ate in the parking lot with the engine on and the heater running, we did our best to catch up on each other's lives.

"I'm sick of all the college talk," Rachel said before biting into her burger. "Mom is on me every night. I only care about going to prom with Joey Reynolds, and I'll be happy if I get into University of Iowa. He's the senior class president. I'm worried he'll ask this blonde girl on the cheerleading squad. She's not even pretty."

I said, "I had my first kiss," and dipped a fry into my ice cream.

"Finally," she said, followed by, "Hold up. There are straight guys at your school?"

"Yes," I said defensively.

"Do you like him?" she asked. "Is he your boyfriend?"

"I can't have a boyfriend right now," I said. "I have no idea what I'm doing next year. My parents insisted on at least five college applications, but I have to get into a ballet company, Rachel. It's the only thing I care about."

"You've wanted it forever, since kindergarten," she said. "You're the only person our age who knows what they want to be when they grow up."

After Rachel dropped me off, I felt sad that our paths diverged more every time I saw her. Mom reassured me that the one thing Rachel and I would always have in common was our whole childhoods.

Accurate as that was, seeing my oldest friend made me realize how much I'd grown since I moved to New York. More significant changes were yet to come.

CHAPTER 11

When I returned to school after winter break, I went to a professional photographer to get my résumé pictures. Most girls in my class went to the same person who did them for SBNY students every year. We needed a variety of images for company auditions.

The photographer took dozens of headshots and different full-body pictures of me in classical poses: *arabesque, passé, grande jété.* I studied the negatives, fascinated to see my appearance, but the photos weren't what I expected. Looking at them made me feel like I didn't know myself. The corrections I repeatedly received in class were obvious: I had raised shoulders, and my back swayed in several shots. My face looked young and fragile.

My friends and I discussed the upcoming company auditions at every meal, and the spring Workshop performances loomed. All except two in the upper-division class were seniors. There was no coming back in the fall for those of us graduating.

The stress was a distraction from my weird feelings before the break, and socially, things returned to normal. The main difference was with Jesse. We were friendlier. For the first time, we partnered in *pas de deux* class.

"I thought about you over winter break," Jesse whispered as we stood behind Charlie and Hilary, waiting our turn to dance the *adagio*.

"Don't flirt with me," I said, secretly pleased.

"Who, me?" he said, and I felt his warm breath on my neck as I looked at our reflection in the mirror.

Jesse took my hand and led me forward. I stepped into a high *arabesque*. Our eyes locked as he faced me, pivoting my body on one toe in a perfect circle. His way of partnering was more sensitive than Tyler's, and he was the strongest guy in the school. I felt so safe in his arms. We looked at each other while we danced, and when we couldn't see each other, I was so conscious of him that I could see him in my mind's eye.

Tyler and I were avoiding each other outside the studio, but when he saw me dancing with Jesse, he asked me to repeat combinations with him, too. We both knew Matthew expected us to go together and favored us as a pair. No matter what was between Tyler and me outside the studio, when we danced, we did a job together that we knew how to do well.

Tyler was like a familiar sweater, but the more I danced with Jesse, the more I felt connected to him, physically and mentally. That was how partnering was supposed to be. There was trust with Jesse that had never been there with any partner I'd ever had. I could have danced with him forever.

Every girl in the upper division took the cattle-call auditions in January and February for San Francisco, Los Angeles, Seattle, and Miami, the other four big companies that performed Roizman ballets. All the directors were former dancers with BNY.

The auditions were just a class, and it was convenient that they all happened right at SBNY, but hundreds of dancers came. The directors made cuts after barre because the studio was too crowded.

The auditions forced everyone into an emotional frenzy but provided few answers. Charles Diamond took my résumé at the end of class. He took Marie's and Nicole's too. I waited every day for a call or a letter, and nothing came.

Los Angeles sent me a rejection three weeks after the audition, and Seattle's no-thank-you came after four. Miami put us through the whole audition and then announced that they weren't hiring, followed by a blanket, "We'll keep you in mind for the future," to the whole room.

Every day, we waited, hoping a director would think of us a week after the audition, change his mind, and decide to call or write. But there was nothing except empty mailboxes, silent phones, and increasing anxiety. The competition was so fierce that we hardly talked to each other.

Only two girls from SBNY, Nicole and Faye, received job offers from the auditions. Marie and I nearly died when Charles offered Nicole an apprenticeship with Ballet San Francisco. She hadn't even attended the San Francisco summer program and wasn't interested in the company.

"I turned him down," Nicole told Charlie in line ahead of me in the cafeteria.

My heart sank. She wouldn't have been so confident turning down San Francisco unless Madame Sivenko had told her she was a shoo-in at BNY.

The offer Faye received surprised everyone. She was still a hard worker who flew under the radar. William Mason offered her an apprenticeship with Los Angeles Ballet Theater.

Faye was one of the girls the teachers also tended to overlook, too, and when she told me her news after pointe class, she said didn't even ask Madame Sivenko if she should hold out for BNY. "SBNY has never treated me like a favorite," she said. "They like me well enough, but I've known since last year that I didn't have a shot with Victor.

When William called, I accepted on the spot. I practically screamed in his ear I was so excited."

After pointe class, when I walked off the elevator to the dorms, Jesse happened to be standing there and hugged me without saying a word. He knew how hard it was.

"Maybe Charles will reconsider after he sees you in Workshop," he said, not caring that I was sweaty.

"As if we aren't all desperate enough," I said, hugging him like a life preserver.

We pulled apart, and I confessed, "Everything after June is a gaping black hole. I'm so worried. I never thought I'd say this, and I still don't want to go, but I'm grateful my parents made me do those college applications."

It felt good to make him laugh.

"Did you get in?" he asked.

"I got accepted to Fordham and my dad's alma mater, the University of Chicago, but I can't wrap my head around college at all," I said. "My parents and I got in a huge fight because I said no to Fordham and asked the University of Chicago if I could defer a year. What are your plans?"

He looked down the hallway in one direction and then the other. "Can I tell you a secret?" he whispered. "I got into UCLA and declined. No one else knows, but Charles offered me a job in San Francisco."

"That's amazing," I said, startled. "Congratulations." I hugged him again, and my envy turned to regret. After June, I'd probably never see him again.

His mind was elsewhere. He pulled away and said, "I was so stressed out. Madame Sivenko talked to Victor before I gave Charles an answer, but Victor said he didn't think I was right for BNY and should take the job in San Francisco. My grandparents are thrilled I'll be back in California."

"That's so great," I said. He'd worked so hard and deserved good news.

He cocked his head and stared me down. "I know what you're thinking—it's easier for guys to get a job—but I came here hoping for BNY too."

He looked vulnerable, but I'd heard the same sob story from Jen and couldn't muster much sympathy. Did he know how much I'd give to have his problems?

Kissing him was tempting. I knew he was thinking about it from how he looked at me. But I knew I'd feel used.

"It sounds like it worked out for the best," I said and stepped around him. "See you later."

If I opened the door for him, I worried he'd only use me to feel better about himself. I was tired of watching boys get whatever they wanted. Giving in would mean surrendering the only power I had.

"Guess what, dancers?" Matthew said at the start of the *pas de deux* class. "Today, I'm looking to see who dances best with whom for Workshop casting."

There was nervous laughter and teasing. "The pressure is on," I whispered, looking up at Jesse. "Who do you want to dance with?"

"The question is, who do *you* want to dance with?" Jesse said. "For once, I'd like to see you figure out what you want."

I rolled my eyes at him, but it was the first time I thought about what it would mean if I made that kind of decision. My life was all about waiting for others to make choices about me.

When Matthew took my hand to demonstrate the combination a moment later, I did my best to play it cool. The other girls' disappointed expressions reminded me to stay humble. We all wanted to be chosen but felt guilty when it happened.

Jesse and I went together for the first few exercises. Matthew challenged us and gave us the most brutal partnering combination we'd ever tried, a mix of jumps, turns, and lifts. I went first with Jesse, and we nailed it. We finished with a clean quadruple *pirouette* right in front of Matthew.

"Very nice," Matthew said. "Anna, will you dance with Tyler for the rest of the class? I'd like to see you two together."

Tyler came and stood next to me. Jesse stepped back. The boys had impeccable manners in the studio. I caught Jesse's eye in the mirror. We knew this was just how it was, but we could feel each other's disappointment.

Matthew looked at Marie. "Let's see you try the lifts across the floor with Jesse."

Marie nodded. Jesse led Marie to the back corner of the studio. He positioned himself behind her, still out of breath from dancing with me.

Matthew gestured to the pianist, and Marie leaped into a split after four counts. Jesse supported her with one hand on her back and one on her waist, boosting her higher and further with each split jump. She stepped into a *piqué ara-besque*, extending one leg high behind her.

Jesse placed his right hand on her right hip and his left hand under her raised left leg. Bending his knees, he hoisted her high over his head and straightened his arms. His face turned red with exertion. I marveled at his endurance as he held her overhead and walked a complete circle to the center of the room.

He bent his knees and elbows, and as he straightened up, he tossed Marie into the air with a slight forward rotation in his wrist. She straightened her right leg next to her left, executing a complete horizontal flip in the air at breakneck speed. We all knew Jesse was supposed to catch her waist and leg, then lower her to a fish dive position with her nose inches from the floor. It was the same trick he'd just done a moment earlier with me.

But Jesse was tired, and he and Marie had no experience dancing together because she always stuck with Jamal. Jesse miscalculated. He threw her a few inches too far away from his body.

A thud like a bass drum filled the studio when Marie hit the floor. She landed flat on her back. Someone shrieked.

The pianist stopped abruptly. Everyone froze, shocked, as Jesse frantically apologized.

"Nice job, Jesse," Hilary said, but Tyler gave her such a fierce look that she clapped her hand over her mouth.

"Always showing your true colors," I said, glaring at her.

I pushed ahead of the gathering dancers and crouched at Marie's side. Her breathing was fast. Jesse hovered over her. He looked terrified.

Matthew squatted next to me. "Don't move," Matthew said to her. "We'll get help." He pointed at Faye and said, "Go immediately to the office and tell them to call an ambulance. Tell the new secretary to call Dr. Westover and ask him to meet Marie at the ER at St. Luke's. Have her call the dorm office, too. They can call her parents."

Fay rushed outside, and Marie opened her eyes. "I want my mom," she said. "It hurts."

"Where?" Jesse asked.

Matter-of-factly, she said, "I felt a snap in my lower back."

I exchanged a look with Matthew.

"I've never dropped anyone, ever," Jesse said, distraught.

"This can't be happening," Marie said, her face pale. Tears trickled down her cheeks.

I felt sick to my stomach. "You're going to be fine," I said, but I wasn't so sure.

Everything was over if she couldn't dance for the next three months. She didn't have a job yet, and they'd take her out of Workshop. It would be the end.

Matthew said, "It's going to be OK."

Marie looked up into his eyes. "No. I don't think it is," she said.

Jesse stood there looking even more upset than Marie. "I'm so sorry," he said over and over. He looked scared.

All I could think was that it could have been me. I was so glad it wasn't me. I felt like a terrible friend for thinking about it, but I was glad it wasn't me.

The next few minutes felt like hours until the paramedics arrived. Very gently, with an air of expertise, they moved Marie onto a stretcher. She only whimpered a little, but I knew the pain was more acute than she let on. She was a tough girl.

We stared in somber silence as they carried her out.

Matthew said, "That's enough for today." He put his arm around Jesse's shoulder and guided him out of the room.

Everyone looked dazed. The last fifteen minutes were surreal.

I tried to imagine how Marie's parents would react to the news and couldn't. They'd sold their *house*. Her family worked so hard to help her follow her dream, yet after all their efforts, her future might come down to a split-second mistake.

I visited Marie three times in the hospital over the next two weeks. "Let's plan my retirement party," she said as I put the flowers I'd brought on her dresser. There was a card from Jesse on a vase of roses.

She'd fractured her spine. Her parents flew in from Paris. The doctors gave her heavy pain medication, put her in a back brace, and told her after a few weeks of rest, she'd start intensive physical therapy.

"When can you dance again?" I asked her.

She laughed. "Wrong question. What you meant to say was, when will I be able to walk normally and get through the day without narcotics?"

Her mother, who was as elegant as Marie, walked me out and explained in her French accent that there were months of rehab ahead. "She will not be dancing the rest of the year."

I wondered how Marie would process it.

"That poor boy, Jesse," said her mom. "He feels so terrible. Marie insists it wasn't his fault, but of course it's his fault."

"It was no one's fault," I said, feeling sorry for everyone involved. "Ballet is hard and risky. It could have happened to any of us."

On my third visit, Marie's mom pulled me aside and said it would be better if I didn't visit for a while. "You remind her of what she's missing," she said in a kind tone. "It's not personal. We're going to move her out of the dorms into an apartment once the hospital releases her. I plan to stay the rest of the school year. Then she can focus on her therapy and still graduate on schedule."

I wondered if Marie had any say in all the decisions.

They posted the casting for Workshop a few days later.

"Congratulations," Faye said when I stood beside her, craning my neck to see the board.

I scanned the *corps de ballet* list but didn't see my name anywhere. Had I not been cast?

Then I saw it. I had to blink. I rubbed my eyes, but it was still there. My name was next to the principal roles in two of the ballets on the program: a short piece called *Waltz* and the final showstopper, *Fire*. "I can't believe it."

Seeing that Nicole and Hilary were also learning the lead in *Fire* and Hilary was my alternate in *Waltz* couldn't stop my heart from bursting with happiness. The boys for *Waltz* were Qi and Charlie and for *Fire,* Jesse, Tyler, and Jamal. They hadn't listed who would partner with whom.

Because they'd cast me in the leads, I had the best-remaining shot at a job. All the artistic directors would see the shows. They couldn't overlook me if I were the only one on the stage.

I glanced at the ocean of troubled faces staring up at the board. The casting was the most honest indication of what the school thought of us. This was no end-of-the-year conference. We'd finally seen how we ranked next to our peers.

"It's confusing," one girl said to another. "We both worked so hard. Why did I only get two minor roles in the *corps de ballet?*"

Rehearsals began the following week. The atmosphere changed. Our purpose was clear, and we had our defined roles.

For *Waltz,* I started with separate rehearsals from the *corps de ballet* to learn the principal role. Madame Sivenko, who used to dance the lead in *Waltz* herself, taught us the steps.

"Anna, you're with Qi," Madame Sivenko directed. That came as a relief. Qi was humble and made his partners look good, which wasn't always the case. Charlie worried about himself, the kiss of death for a successful partnership.

That meant Hilary and Charlie were together. They were already arguing. "Could you please put lotion on your hands?" she said to him. "They feel like sandpaper."

He turned red. "Only if you stop bathing in perfume."

Madame Sivenko waved us over to the TV cart. "Let's watch the video," she said, and when she hit play, there was a young version of her flying across the stage. I knew her reputation and had seen pictures, but what I saw on the screen made her expertise real to me in a completely new way. I recognized her unique qualities in the video: the way she tilted her head or gestured with her arms was the same as when she taught our class, even though she hadn't danced a ballet in at least twenty years. But I had never envisioned her with so much youthful energy. I was inspired.

"This ballet is like high-impact aerobics," Madame Sivenko said, talking over the video. "There's fast footwork and you need every ounce of energy. Hilary and Anna, you only have a three-minute rest during the twelve-minute piece. The rest is go-go-go. That will be challenging because, in class, we stop in between combinations. You're strong and have good technique, which is why I cast you, but you don't have a lot of stamina. You'll see the first time we run the whole ballet."

She wasn't kidding. By the end of rehearsal, Hilary and I were huffing and puffing like old ladies, and we'd only learned the first variation. It was a wake-up call. Getting the role was only the first step. I had to master it and had a long way to go before I could dance the choreography full-out at performance level.

Nicole, Jesse, Hilary, Jamal, Tyler, and I stood by the door at the first *Fire* rehearsal.

Vivienne walked in with a clipboard. "Anna, you're with Tyler," she said. It made sense even though I wanted Jesse. Hilary and Nicole needed the taller partners.

Partnering together came naturally to Tyler and me, just as our friendship had. Maybe this would be a good way to mend it. This was our happy place, where the issues outside the studio faded away.

He took my hand and said, "Let's stand in the center."

I let him lead me forward, but it felt strange to be starting such a big endeavor with him after the weirdness of the past few months.

Jesse looked friendly with Nicole, but Jamal had an annoyed look on his face after Vivienne put him with Hilary. He had to have been thinking about Marie.

A petite, dark-haired woman about my mom's age appeared in the door. She wore a jogging suit and sneakers, and her face was makeup-free. Her magnetic presence had an immediate impact on the energy in the room. A light seemed to shine out of her in every direction. Vivienne beckoned to her to come in, and they embraced. I recognized her.

"That's Stacy Hannah," I said.

"Wow," Tyler said. "She left the company about twenty years ago." We looked at each other. I thought of the first time we saw the company dance *Fire* together. That was the night he'd said we should dance it together.

"Does she still live in New York?" I asked.

"I doubt it," Tyler said. "She's never been back here, as far as I know. She's one of those people who checked out and focused on family after her retirement," Tyler said.

Vivienne turned to us. "I doubt Stacy Hannah needs an introduction," she announced. "We're so fortunate she's here to teach you the role she originated in *Fire*."

Stacy scanned the room while Vivienne talked, locking gazes with each of us. Her eyes were huge and intelligent.

"They're all yours," Vivienne said to Stacy. Vivienne winked at me and sat in a chair, looking as curious as the rest of us. It was cool to see my teacher act like a student.

Stacy clasped her hands together. "Thanks for having me, Vivienne. When Nicholas choreographed *Fire*—I'll date myself, but I think it was close to thirty years ago—we had no idea if the ballet would succeed. All we knew was how exciting it was to have a Roizman choreograph a ballet for us. William used to say dancing the ballet gave him a rush."

I smiled, and Stacy looked right at me but didn't smile back. Her eyes were sharp as bullets.

Stacy continued, "Because the choreography is unconventional, it can look like improvisation to the audience, but everything is deliberate. The *pas de deux* is often described as representing the complexity of a romantic relationship. You must trust each other. Gentlemen, your partner needs to know you'll be there to catch her when she takes all those risks: falling, jumping across the stage, you know what I mean."

My eyes moved from my reflection to Jesse, still berating himself about Marie. He hadn't been himself since her accident.

His eyes shifted to mine in the mirror.

We spent the next two hours in thrall to Stacy, practicing the most difficult sections of the *pas de deux*. Tyler and I lost ourselves in the work. We found the right tension in our grip so he could support me while I kicked, turned, jumped, fell, and flew. His hands moved expertly from my waist to my hands to my back to my legs. He lifted me over his head and caught me as I fell.

Vivienne watched us make mistakes and said, "You're going to practice this a lot before June."

"Good, you two," Stacy said when we executed one of the problematic lifts successfully for the first time, the first couple to get it right. I smiled at Tyler, but he looked past me in the mirror.

Why was it easy to connect with him when we danced? If only real life felt so simple.

Once we'd learned all the steps in *Waltz*, Madame Sivenko made each cast run the complete ballet without stopping. Hilary watched my every move. Her competitiveness motivated me to push past my exhaustion, but it also invited Madame Sivenko to compare us.

"Did you notice how nicely Hilary runs on for her variation, Anna?" Madame Sivenko called without ever taking her eyes off Hilary's run-thru. I watched from the side, inwardly cringing.

Qi shot me a sympathetic glance from across the room.

A few minutes later, Charlie and Hilary struggled through a partnering sequence, and Madame Sivenko told them to watch me demonstrate it with Qi.

The comparisons weighed on Hilary, too, so much so that we started swapping knowing glances every time Madame Sivenko pitted us against each other.

Hilary approached me at the end of rehearsal. "Will you go over the end of the variation with me?" she asked. "I missed the rehearsal when we learned the counts, and I'm having trouble with the phrasing."

We went over the sequence several times.

Afterward, she picked up her bag. "Thanks," she said.

It almost sounded like she meant it.

CHAPTER 12

The days flew by because of all the rehearsals, and before I knew it, May arrived.

I walked to Marie's apartment. So much had changed in the two months since her accident. She'd called me a few times, but there wasn't much to say, and she never wanted to get together. From what I gathered from Jamal, she talked to him much more than to me. I'd been surprised when she'd invited me over.

"It's good to see you," she said when she opened the door. We hugged each other. To my relief, the old Marie was still in there, the part of her I'd grown to know and love that had nothing to do with dance. We sat by the window, and she showed me her back brace.

Her mom brought us a plate of macaroons. Marie seemed like a different person when she put one in her mouth. The old Marie wouldn't have touched dessert if it were the last food on earth.

"Tell me about rehearsals," she said.

I relaxed. "*Waltz* is killing me. Hilary said she has tendonitis and started sitting out, which means I've had to dance with Charlie's cast in addition to mine. At least my stamina is getting better, but it's so hard. I can't tell how much she's faking it."

"Do you think Hilary will get into BNY?" Marie asked, tucking her blonde hair behind her ears.

I didn't want to think about it. "Nicole's the one I think will get in. How's your back?"

"Better, but I'm still miles away from normal," she said. "I have physical therapy all the time."

I wanted to ask her about her plans for the future but didn't dare.

She bit into another cookie. As if she could read my mind, she said, "I'll do therapy all summer, and in the fall, I'm going to Columbia."

"Columbia University?"

She'd already decided. College?

"Everyone in BNY is miserable anyway," she said.

I wondered how much of that was fear she wouldn't be able to dance again and how much of that was true. "But they made it," I said. "They're living the dream."

"Making it isn't the end," she said. "Whatever we do next is just the beginning. Ballet companies might be too much like dictatorships for me."

I raised my eyebrows, but I knew what she meant. It wasn't for everyone.

She leaned forward, her green eyes glowing. "College isn't a death sentence. Why do we think cutting ourselves off from other things is noble? There is no pension or job security in American ballet. We think all we need is dance, but when I was lying there in the hospital, I realized I wanted ballet to be part of my life, not my whole life."

I stood and walked over to the bookcase, feeling sorry for her, and thinking how strange it was that she felt sorry for me.

There was a framed picture of Marie and her parents standing in front of the Eiffel Tower.

"Can I come visit you in Paris someday?" I asked.

She laughed, a sound I loved and hadn't heard in ages. "You better."

When I climbed in bed at night, I cleared away my worries by thinking through the steps to *Fire*. My mind rehearsed constantly, in my dreams and during every spare moment of the day. Jen shook me awake in the middle of the night on more than one occasion because I was correcting myself out loud. I kept practicing in my sleep. Once, I kicked the wall so hard that I woke her up.

All six of us danced simultaneously, but Tyler and I received most of Stacy's attention in her rehearsals. She wanted something so particular from us, a language beyond words. Her voice was in my head. Vivienne would jump in sometimes and have Stacy correct Nicole, Jesse, Hilary, and Jamal, but Tyler and I were her favorites.

"Today, let's have each couple run the entire *pas de deux* alone," Stacy announced. "The rest of you, come up front and watch." Jesse and Nicole volunteered to go first.

Hilary, Jamal, Tyler, and I sat on the floor beside Vivienne.

Jesse and Nicole took their places and Stacy signaled to the pianist. After practicing the individual lifts and particular steps separately so many times, it was exciting to connect them, like instead of practicing a note we could finally sing the song. Jesse expertly guided Nicole through the *pas de deux*.

Stacy let them run the entire piece without stopping. It had a traditional structure. First the boy and girl danced together at a slower pace, then the boy had a solo, the girl had a solo, and then they danced together again.

Nicole looked good in the part. I studied the way her body moved and thought about how I could learn from her.

"Next?" Stacy called after giving Jesse and Nicole a few brief corrections. Hilary and Jamal volunteered.

They had more difficulty. Their timing with each other was off. Jamal was awkward, and Hilary was irritated. Their rehearsal frustrated everyone. Stacy went over a few of the trouble spots, but the overarching issue—that they couldn't connect—wasn't easy to fix.

We were next. Tyler pulled me to my feet and led me out onto the floor.

I struck the opening pose, and Tyler stepped behind me. He held one of my hands and supported my back with his other hand.

On the first note, I bent my left leg, still on pointe, and let my right leg fly out behind me in a powerful kick. We watched our reflections. Tyler's expression was as intense as my own.

The *adagio* ended with a difficult turn. I pushed off his arm, and he stepped away, letting me whip my leg around and spin as many times as possible. The turn made me nervous because I messed it up often, but I was so full of adrenaline that I hit a perfect triple and sustained the ending. Jamal whistled as I ran off the floor.

Tyler danced his variation while I tried to catch my breath. His solo didn't last nearly long enough, and I was back on for my variation before I had my breathing under control. Everyone focused their energy on me. I flew through the steps, counting to stay precisely on the music.

My variation ended, and we repeated the opening, moving toward the final moments in the *pas de deux*. I could feel Tyler's exhaustion as much as mine. We mentally pushed each other, willing ourselves to the end. His sweat ran down my skin. I felt his heart beating.

On the final phrase of the music, I ran toward him and took a flying leap. I'd never felt so alive as I did in that moment. He caught me, abruptly stopping my forward motion, and pulled me backward from the jump. My nose nearly touched the floor as my legs wrapped back around his head. We struck the final pose just as the music ended.

There was a moment of silence. Tyler lifted me up and placed me back on my feet.

"Good," Stacy said. "Let's talk about a few things." She walked over to us. "Show me the pull-away."

Tyler took my hands, breathing hard, and we returned to one of the trickier sections. Stacy coached us into trying the step in a riskier and more off-balance way. The moment was immediately better.

I remembered when I thought I'd never be able to dance something so complicated. That seemed like a long time ago.

"Enough for today," Stacy said. "Great work, everyone."

CHAPTER 13

The assistant dorm director helped me make a podiatrist appointment, and the address was a brownstone on the Upper East Side. I skipped French class and took a cab across Central Park early on a Tuesday morning, desperate for foot relief from my corns and an ingrown toenail. The Workshop was less than a month away.

After my appointment, I walked outside and came face-to-face with Stacy Hannah. She wore a royal blue blouse with slacks and sneakers. How was she even more striking outside ballet? We stood on the tree-lined street, just two regular people in the real world.

"Anna," she said, her voice warm. There was something both so kind and no-nonsense about her.

I was thrilled she recognized me outside the studio.

"Are you OK?" she asked.

I realized she was as surprised as I was that we'd run into each other in a different neighborhood. I told her about my foot issues, and she nodded sympathetically.

"I'm on my way back from an appointment, too," she said, and I wondered what it was for. "Let me walk you closer to the park." Her eyes were more penetrating than ever, studying me as I fell in step with her. After a silence, she said, "What are your plans for next year?"

The question was like a punch in the gut. "I still need a job."

"Have they said anything to you about BNY?" she asked.

"Not exactly." I was embarrassed to admit it. "They've implied I'm too short, though."

She nodded knowingly. "Did you audition for Los Angeles? You're William's type. I think he'd love you."

Her compliment was the nicest thing anyone had said to me in the almost two years I'd been in New York, mainly because it came from her.

I explained that I'd auditioned for Los Angeles in February and didn't get in, but William hadn't been there. The ballet mistress and the resident choreographer ran the audition.

"Something will work out," she said, hailing me a cab. "You're doing great in *Fire*. Keep that energy and personality in your dancing. Unfortunately, I won't be at any more of the rehearsals."

I couldn't hide my disappointment. "Why not?"

"We're heading to San Francisco. My husband is speaking at a conference, and I'll be staging *America* for Charles Diamond.

I won't be back in New York until the end of the summer. I'm so sorry I won't see the Workshop performances. You've worked so hard. I'm sure Vivienne will tell me all about it."

I couldn't believe she was going to miss the show.

"Don't worry," she said, touching my shoulder. "I already know you'll be great."

She held the door for me as I climbed into the cab. I waved at her as it pulled away from the curb.

It was the type of interaction a young dancer never forgets, and as the years went by, that conversation with Stacy crystallized in my mind as one of the most meaningful moments in my life.

Vivienne conferred with the pianist at the end of *Fire* rehearsal the following week. As I put my bag over my shoulder and walked toward the door, she called, "Anna, I need to speak with you."

Hilary jumped up and hurried out of the door, which struck me as odd. She was usually the nosy type. Jesse, Jamal, Nicole, and Tyler stared openly as I approached Vivienne.

Vivienne leaned forward on the piano and said in a voice too low for the others to hear, "You don't need to come to *Fire* rehearsals anymore. There are only three performances: Hilary will have two, and Nicole will have one. You'll get two shows of *Waltz*, so focus on that."

My heart pounded faster. "I don't understand," I said.

She said the following words slowly as if speaking to a toddler. "We're taking you out of *Fire*."

I gaped at her, floored. Her face was devoid of expression as if she'd removed herself from what she was saying.

I couldn't believe what I'd heard, yet I nodded. I nodded, even though I felt like screaming. Why didn't they do this before I'd spent months rehearsing and anticipating? I'd have given up *Waltz* in a heartbeat to perform *Fire*. Why did Hilary need two shows? Why were they taking me out? Stacy herself said I looked great.

Vivienne picked up her notebook. Her shoulders sagged as she walked past me out the door.

I covered my face and took a deep breath to get myself together. My hands were shaking. When I turned around, Jesse, Jamal, Nicole, and Tyler lingered in the doorway. "What was that about?" Tyler asked.

I walked over to them. "They took me out. You get to dance *Fire* with Hilary."

Tyler's eyes widened in surprise.

"I can't believe it," I said, meeting Jesse's gaze. He looked furious on my behalf.

"At least you still have *Waltz*," Nicole said. She unpinned her long dark hair and let it fall to her shoulders.

"*Waltz* is much shorter and in the middle of the program," Jesse said. "It's not the same as *Fire*."

I wondered why Nicole was still there.

"Why did they cut you?" Jamal asked.

"I don't know," I said. "Vivienne said I should focus on *Waltz*. Tyler and I have been talking about dancing *Fire* together for two years. I can't believe we won't get to perform it." I searched his eyes for an answer he didn't have.

Nicole coughed. What did she want? Wasn't this enough of a triumph for her? Why did she need to hang around and pretend she cared?

"I think you deserve to know something," Nicole said, biting her lip. Jesse crossed his arms and turned to look at her.

"What?" I asked.

"Hilary . . ." she started, biting her lip.

"Hilary?" Tyler asked.

"Hilary's parents donated a million dollars to the school," Nicole said, "and they let Madame Sivenko know how much they'd like to see Hilary have two performances of *Fire*."

My head exploded in a rush of anger. "Why are you telling me?" I asked. "I don't want to know this information."

"She told you that?" Jesse asked.

"That girl," Tyler said, shaking his head. "I don't want to dance with her instead of Anna."

"Tell me about it," Jamal said.

Nicole shrugged. "She has issues." Her eyes fixed on mine. "You looked better. Everyone here knows it. But welcome to the real world. People do what they have to do to get ahead. I just thought you deserved to know."

Jesse rubbed my shoulder as I told Nicole, "I thought Hilary was your friend."

Nicole gave a bitter laugh. "I don't have friends," she said, which seemed like a painful thing to say.

The world didn't stop because I lost my dream role. Instead, time rushed forward faster as the performances approached. I did the only thing I could. I threw myself into my role in *Waltz*.

There was no one to talk to about my disappointment. My parents couldn't understand. Marie was too removed. Jen acted sympathetic, but after almost eight months in National Ballet Theatre, my school issues were childish in her eyes. Jesse and Tyler couldn't relate. The other girls in my class had no sympathy for me.

After Jen fell asleep at night, I'd sit on my windowsill in the dark, looking down at the deserted plaza and wishing for things that would never happen.

For the first time in two years, my parents came to New York. Mom ran up to hug me when I met her and Dad outside their hotel. "You look so grown up," she said, and I remembered that I was something other than a dancer. I was a daughter.

I teared up when Dad put his arms around me. He had on the same blue jacket he'd had since I was a little kid.

We went out to dinner. Seeing them was different than when I went home. This was my world.

Mom, in her new green dress and makeup, beamed with happiness. Dad made a toast and said, "We're so proud of you."

As we sipped our drinks, they exchanged glances. "We have some news," Mom said.

I put my glass down, knowing what she would say before she said it. "Is it the house? You said you were considering selling it in December."

"We didn't want you to worry, especially if it didn't sell," Dad said.

My childhood flashed before my eyes. Riding my bike up and down the street. Painting my bedroom walls purple. Baking cookies with Mom. Birthday parties in the yard. Sitting at the computer with Dad. Reading in the cozy chair by the fireplace. Walking to Rachel's.

"Our agent listed it a week ago," Mom said, "and we assumed it would take a while, so we planned to tell you in person, but it sold in three days. I'm still in shock."

My head hurt. "Where will you go?"

"We bought a condo near the university," Dad said. "There's a spare room for when you come home to visit. Has there been any news about a job?"

The waiter served our food. Even with the ground shifting under my feet, dinner with my parents was still the most comforting place.

Mom put her napkin on her lap and said, "If nothing happens, you can come home and help us move. I'm sure Margaret will give you a job helping with summer dance camps."

I put my hands over my ears and made a face. The thought of it made me want to cry.

"You can take classes at the community college and then transfer credits to the University of Chicago the next year," Dad said. "It'll work out."

The performances were in the Roizman building's street-level theater. On the opening night, a Friday, Faye sat beside me in the dressing room. We checked each other's makeup. I wore a blue tracksuit over my pink tights to keep warm.

"Are you nervous?" I asked.

She stopped applying lipstick and said, "Not like you are." Her mind was already past SBNY, filled with plans for her new life at the Los Angeles Ballet Theater.

Hilary was across the room, putting her makeup on for *Fire.* "I wonder if Victor will offer contracts tonight or wait until the end of the run," she said to the girl beside her, loud enough for the entire room to hear. "Everyone who's anyone is in the audience: Broadway producers, journalists, critics, patrons, movie stars, principal dancers from NBT and BNY, famous choreographers, and every prominent artistic director."

Faye looked at me, and we rolled our eyes.

To everyone's surprise, Madame Sivenko appeared in the dressing room.

"Where's Anna?" she said, looking around. Her gray hair was styled as smooth as her silk dress. I'd never seen her so made up, and she looked beautiful.

I waved from across the room, feeling everyone's eyes on us.

"Let me pin your hairpiece for *Waltz,*" she said. She walked over and picked up the cap of tiny rhinestones next to my makeup case.

"One sec," I said. She watched me close my lipstick. The others turned their attention back to the mirrors.

In the reflection, I watched Madame Sivenko examine my French twist with her typical eagle eye. She placed the headpiece exactly how she wanted it, arranging every rhinestone as if it came straight from Van Cleef and Arpels.

"I loved dancing this ballet," she said. Her voice sounded wistful. "Hand me some pins." I passed her a bobby pin, and she pushed it into my hair as if my head were a pincushion. After a few minutes, she smiled, satisfied with her handiwork.

"Thank you," I said.

"You remind me of myself sometimes," she said, patting my shoulder. I wondered what she meant by that but was too scared to ask.

She said encouraging words to the others and then swept out the door with, "Have a wonderful show, everyone."

We looked around at each other, stunned.

"I didn't know she could be that nice," Faye said.

When the stage manager gave the five-minute call over the intercom, I put on my pointe shoes and left the dressing room. As I walked into the backstage area to warm up, I could hear the rumble in the house. The audience was arriving.

The opening ballet was *Violins*, a classic Roizman piece with eight women and one lead couple. Faye, dressed in a black leotard and pink tights, and Jamal, in a white leotard and black tights, danced the *pas de deux*. I watched from the wings and let the violin concerto be my warm-up music.

It was almost my turn.

CHAPTER 14

When *Violins* was over, I returned to the dressing room to trade my tracksuit for my costume, a long lavender tutu with delicate rhinestones embroidered on the bodice. I checked the mirror to make sure every detail was in place. The skirt came just below my knees, and the skin-colored elastic over my shoulders made the top look strapless.

There was no one around to hook the back of the bodice closed, so I went downstairs with the back of my costume hanging open. One of the girls in the *corps de ballet* of *Violins* was in the hall. She fastened the hooks for me.

Only in the last two weeks did I have enough stamina to dance all of *Waltz* full out. As I tested some of my jumps and turns on the stage, I thought of how the first time I ran the entire ballet, I was so spent by the end that all I could do was stumble around, marking the final steps. Now, I'd learned the moments in the choreography when I could catch my breath.

"Places, please," the stage manager announced. Qi appeared, wearing white tights and a lavender tunic that matched my tutu.

"You look ready to go," I said. Qi kissed my cheek and led me to the back wing.

The eight *corps de ballet* girls formed a diagonal line on the stage. They looked identical with the same hairdos, the same pink costumes, and the same body types.

The orchestra played the overture. A small crowd of other students gathered in the wings to watch. As the curtain rose, the girls danced the opening steps.

I rubbed my hands together and took a deep breath.

"Ready?" Qi asked. He put one hand on my waist and offered me his other. I squeezed his fingers, and we ran out onto the stage.

The bright lights shined right in my eyes. We danced the short opening and ran off, already breathing hard. I bent over in the wings to catch my breath, but there was only a second before my next entrance.

I ran back onstage and danced my first solo. As the music finished, I nailed my final *piqué arabesque* balance. The audience broke into applause. I ran off as Qi began his solo.

I'd never performed for such a critical audience. The shows I did in Rock Island were mainly for family and friends, but in New York, having my parents out there for support was a lifeline.

Before I knew it, I was racing through the finale, trying desperately to feel my feet and push past the exhaustion. The curtain fell after my final leap. The audience broke into applause. A minute later, I was taking my place onstage for the bow.

The curtain rose and Qi led me forward to the audience. How was it over already? My right hand came to my heart as I kneeled and bowed my head in a *grande révérance*.

A voice that sounded like my dad's yelled, "Bravo!" Out of the corner of my eye, I saw Tyler and Jesse clapping in the wings.

When the curtain fell, Qi hugged me, and I walked offstage. Vivienne and Madame Sivenko hurried toward me.

"Very nice," said Madame Sivenko.

Vivienne said, "Good job."

Performing made me happy, but that look in my teachers' eyes meant success. They knew better than anyone how hard I'd worked and how far I'd come. Their approval meant everything.

Jesse picked me up by the waist and twirled me around. "You did it," he said.

At that moment, Victor Caldwell appeared on the side of the stage, and as he walked toward me, my stomach dropped.

Jesse backed away. Maybe this would be my moment after all. I'd danced well. Perhaps I still had a chance.

Madame Sivenko and Vivienne whispered to each other and stared at Victor. From their expressions, I could tell they also thought something was about to happen.

"Wonderful performance of *Waltz*," Victor said in my general direction. "There's someone I need to speak to." He glanced around the stage.

I stepped forward.

"Qi," Victor said, passing me. "May I have a moment?" He took Qi's arm and led him a few feet away, and I stood there, crushed, as Victor made someone else's dream come true.

Vivienne put her hand on my shoulder. "You've worked very hard," she said.

That was when I fully understood that I would never get into Ballet New York. Until that moment, as much as I knew my height was against me, I'd held out a kernel of hope.

I'd given everything I had—my best effort—but my best would never be good enough to make my dreams come true. I'd pinned my hopes on something impossible.

I went to the dressing room to remove my makeup and trade my *Waltz* costume for jeans, a T-shirt, and sneakers.

When I returned to the wings, the lights were up for *Fire,* and the dancers were getting into their places. Tyler and Hilary practiced the spin-away turn at the end of the *pas de deux*. He looked handsome in his scarlet tunic and white tights, and she matched him in a red leotard and skirt. I stood back in the shadows, admiring them. Tyler came over.

"Hey," he said, putting his arms around my waist. "You were great. I'm sorry we're not doing this together."

"Thanks," I said, but I couldn't look him in the eyes. Once Victor gave him his contract with BNY, our lives would go in different directions.

"You've always been a good friend to me," he said. "I may not be the person you want, but I want you to know that I believed in you the first day I met you, and I believe in you now."

I blinked, surprised. He kissed my cheek and jogged back across the stage to find Hilary.

The music began, and the curtain went up. *Fire* floated before my eyes. Despite how the ballet triggered mixed emotions, it rooted deeper into my heart every time I watched it.

Tyler was breathtaking, and Hilary danced beautifully. Only I cared that she was cold. They were young and energetic—the future of ballet.

She was radiant when they took their bows, basking in her good fortune with Tyler by her side.

Before I left, I saw Victor do the same thing to Hilary he'd done to me. He walked right past her and offered Tyler a company apprenticeship.

Leaving the theater was a relief. My parents were waiting in front after the show, holding hands. Dad presented me with a big bouquet.

Mom said, "I always knew you were a beautiful dancer, but seeing you up there blew us away." Her eyes teared up.

I could tell from the look on Dad's face and his body language that something had changed for him, too.

"Did you like the rest of the show?" I asked them as they walked me back to the dorms.

"We're so proud," Mom said. I noticed a stack of programs sticking out of her bag.

"The program was great," Dad said, "but that's not what we came from Rock Island to see." He put a hand on my shoulder and turned me to face him. "We came because we love you. You mean more to us than any performance. Do you realize what's so important about what you achieved? It isn't getting into Ballet New York or being better than anyone else. What matters is that you had a dream, and you fulfilled it. That's a rare thing."

We hugged goodbye. I walked into the building. The lobby was silent as I pressed the button for the elevator.

The doors opened, but before I walked in, I glanced outside. My parents were just two silhouettes. They walked away from me into the night, trusting their love would lift me toward whatever I was meant to become.

Jen was in the room when I came home, exhausted after her own performance. She crawled into bed. "How did it go?" she asked.

"Fine," I said. "I'm tired. How was *Swan Lake*?"

"Not too bad," she said. "I just haven't figured out how to stop my calves from cramping when we stand in that line through the whole *pas de deux*. But it's OK."

She was so lucky to dance in NBT's legendary production of *Swan Lake*. What was that even like? She was in a whole other world.

"I have the matinee off on Sunday," she said, "so if I can get out at the half-hour call, I can see your last performance of *Waltz*."

"It's not that big a deal," I lied, desperately wanting her to come. "But I'd love it if you can."

She sat up in bed and looked at me. "I want to cheer you on. That's what friends do."

"Thanks, Jen." She'd made *me* a better person since the day we met. I flipped the light off and crawled into bed. "By the way, did you hear that Qi and Tyler got into BNY today?"

"They did?" she asked in the darkness, and I heard a trace of regret in her voice. "I hadn't heard."

We bonded over it without saying a word, even though she was past letting go of that dream. Jen started to snore, and even though I was exhausted, I lay awake for a long time.

On Saturday, I had a quick breakfast in the cafeteria with my parents before they went off to a matinee of *Tosca*.

"Are you sure you can't come with us to the opera?" Dad asked. "We could still try to get you a ticket."

"I need to start packing," I said. "You go enjoy. The school said we're expected at the theater later even if we're not performing. They need us on standby to cover in case something happens at the last minute."

Later that afternoon, I went to the theater to sign in as Hilary's alternate.

"You're not in the show either, right?" Tyler asked me backstage.

He looked cuter than ever. "Good detective work," I said. "That's why we're the only ones in street clothes."

To my surprise, he slung his arm around my shoulder. "Want to sit in the audience together, like old times?"

I let him guide me through the door that led to the lobby. In the theater, we gossiped about all the celebrities in the audience, and he told me that Charlie had accepted a job offer from Boston.

Hilary and Charlie gave an excellent performance of *Waltz*. As I watched, I wished that Marie could have been the one to share the part with me. She'd said on the phone that she wasn't planning to attend the Workshop performances, and I didn't blame her.

When the lights came down for *Fire*, Tyler looked over at me. We had to let things be, whatever they were. I smiled at him.

The curtain went up. Dancers twirled across the stage, pristine in their red costumes. Thanks to Stacy's coaching, Nicole and Jesse came onstage with energy, expertly performing each step. Even though Tyler and I weren't dancing the ballet together, we gripped each other's hands, sharing the same love for it.

After the show ended and I split off from Tyler, I ran into Vivienne and Simon standing outside the theater door.

Vivienne looked stunning in a powder-blue skirt, a gauzy blouse, and jeweled flats. Simon wore a navy jacket and a bow tie. They had such an air of importance about them. I knew I was privileged to study under them for so long. They'd taught me when to fight. They'd taught me when just to let things be. They'd taught me to let my mind be quiet to know myself.

"Are your parents in town?" Vivienne asked, showing more interest in me than she ever had before.

"Yes, thanks," I said, "I'm so glad they could be here."

"That's wonderful," Simon said.

"I'm so sad to be almost done," I said, gathering up my courage, "And Vivienne, I guess you were right when we talked last year. I probably will go to college, even after all of this."

She and Simon stared at me. There was a comfortable silence, maybe because I had nothing to prove. We'd all done everything we could.

Vivienne put her hand on my shoulder and looked me in the eyes. Her mouth turned up in a smile. "Anna," she said. "I can't predict the future. I don't know what's going to happen. But I watch dancers every day, and I can see so much about your personalities by how you dance. Let me say, I don't think it's over for you yet."

Simon nodded wisely.

My lower lip trembled as I watched them disappear into the crowd. I put a hand on my forehead. My skin felt warm, and I was sweating. Maybe I was more nervous about the last show than I'd realized.

Jen had already left for company class when I woke up. I'd overslept. The warm-up class started in less than an hour.

Although I was never sick, my forehead was burning up. When I climbed out of bed, I stumbled and was so dizzy that I collapsed on the floor.

After a minute, I collected myself. I took pain medication and hurried to the studio.

"Last day, everyone," Charlie called as dancers took their barre spots and pulled on their shoes.

"You're fine, you're fine," I coached myself. But I wasn't fine. There was no way around it.

Madame Sivenko walked in and gestured to the pianist. We started our *pliés,* and I focused on the familiar movements. "Come on. Come on, body," I said.

It wasn't working. I was shaky and weak. Usually if I didn't feel great before class, dancing made me feel better, but this was different. The more I danced the worse I felt.

I stood in the back of the room when everyone came to the center, afraid that if I let go of the barre I'd pass out.

"Are you all right?" Hilary asked with genuine concern in her voice.

"I've felt better," I admitted, immediately regretting it. Hilary's presence brought up years of anger and resentment. It unnerved me that she, of all people, took notice. She would probably love it if she had to cover my last performance of *Waltz.*

Madame Sivenko wasn't even bothering to correct us. She wouldn't notice if I skipped some combinations or took it easy. A voice in my head whispered, "What does this last performance even matter?" The year was over. It would have already happened if someone planned to offer me a job.

But when class ended, Madame Sivenko marched right over to me. Why did I think she wouldn't notice that I was off? She saw everything, especially if it was something we wanted to hide.

"You look terrible," she said. "What's going on?" She touched my forehead. "You're burning up."

We weren't supposed to show weakness. We weren't supposed to complain. We weren't supposed to have injuries. We weren't supposed to get sick.

No fever was going to wreck my last chance to get onstage.

"I'm just a little rundown, but I'm fine," I insisted. Hilary lingered a few feet away and caught my eye.

"There's no need to be a hero," Madame Sivenko said, appraising me from head to toe.

"I said I'm fine," I repeated, picking up my bag. "I need to get over to the theater."

Madame Sivenko saw the determined look on my face and said, "OK, then."

I had the chills while I applied my makeup and put on my pointe shoes. People spoke to me in the dressing room, and my head throbbed so much I had no idea what they were saying. I did my hair in a daze. Every minute, I felt worse.

Once I was ready, I found a dark corner backstage to stretch. Tyler appeared in his costume for *Violins* and caught my eye as he walked past. I wanted to tell him what was happening but felt too exhausted. He walked over to where Hilary and Jamal stood laughing a few feet away. The sound hurt my ears.

The dancers in *Violins* gathered onstage. After two shows, there was less nervousness and more anticipation. The lights went down, the curtain rose, and the music began. I walked into the wing to watch Tyler.

Hilary approached me. She was in her warmups, getting ready for *Fire*. "You still look sick," she whispered. "Should I put my costume on for *Waltz*, just in case?"

"I can't make you dance two ballets in a row," I said, gripping the boom with the stage lights so tightly my knuckles turned white.

What I didn't say that she already knew was, "This performance is everything to me. It might be the last performance I ever get."

"I don't mind," Hilary said.

"I said I'm fine."

"I'm trying to help you," she said, spitting the word *help*.

"I don't need—" I started, but Jesse suddenly stepped between us. His performances were over, and he was in his street clothes.

"Hilary said you're sick?" he asked.

I turned my head away from him. He put his hand to my forehead.

"Wow," he said, "you're running some fever."

I backed away from him.

He took my arm and said, "Maybe it wouldn't hurt for Hilary to put on the other costume and stand in the wings."

When I didn't respond, she said, "Thank you, Jesse," and hurried triumphantly off toward the dressing rooms.

I closed my eyes and took a deep breath.

"I didn't mean to take Hilary's side," Jesse said. "You feel scary hot, though. Do you honestly think you can dance?"

"You don't understand," I said, pushing past him. "Leave me alone."

As the curtain fell on *Violins*, I hurried back to the alcove behind the stage to get a drink from the water fountain. Everything was dark in the back, but I knew where to go without the lights. I drank and drank until I could barely breathe, afraid my mouth would go dry while I was onstage. When I came up for air, cold rushed to my head. I staggered backward and stumbled into a trash can.

As the stage manager called, "Five minutes. Five minutes, please," over the loudspeaker, I turned and vomited into the garbage.

It was time to go on.

Qi approached me as soon as I appeared backstage. "Should we try a lift?" he asked.

My mind was blank. "I've forgotten the entire ballet."

He gave me a nervous look. "Impossible. We rehearsed *Waltz* for two months."

But for my life, I couldn't think of the choreography. The steps would have to come back when I heard the music. That's why we practiced so much. My body would know what to do.

Qi walked over to the side to rub rosin into his hands; they had slipped on my waist in the *promenade* on Friday night. The rosin would help his hands stick to the satin on my costume.

He led me to the wing when the music began. My head pounded. He put one hand on my waist and offered me the other. The *corps de ballet* danced their opening steps, and we ran onto the stage.

The lights disoriented me. Jesse appeared in the front wing, and I saw Hilary standing behind him, wearing her identical *Waltz* costume. The sight was so upsetting that I stumbled and rushed to recover.

Qi lifted me across the stage and placed me down in *arabesque*. Somehow, I danced. At the end of the opening, he guided me off into the wing.

"You remembered the steps," he said, putting his hands on his knees and leaning over to breathe. It was the point in the ballet when we always gasped for air, but this was worse than ever before. I couldn't get air back into my lungs.

Onstage, the *corps de ballet* moved from pattern to pattern. I ran around the wing and back onto the stage for my first solo. The girls cleared as I traveled across the stage, my feet racing through the footwork on autopilot. I could hardly feel my body. Dancers were such a contradiction. There I was, leaping and smiling while my feet were bleeding and my heart was breaking.

Three people gathered in the front wing across from Jesse and Hilary. To my surprise, the figures were Jen and Marie, standing next to Tyler. He was still wearing his *Violins* costume.

Imbued with their energy and touched by the unexpected support, I kept going.

With my best friends there, despite everything, I tuned into how beautiful the music was and felt the melody through every inch of my body. The stage and audience were mine. I did what I'd trained my whole life to do.

At the end of the variation, I whipped out a triple *pirouette*. The audience broke into applause.

I stepped forward to bow. The world spun, and the lights were so bright that I almost pitched forward into the orchestra pit.

Somehow, I ran into the wing toward my best friends, stumbling, my legs buckling beneath me. The orchestra picked up the music and continued.

Jen reached forward to catch me as the world went black.

CHAPTER 15

The next thing I heard was applause.

Someone pressed a wet towel to my face. I pushed the hand away to protect my makeup and opened my eyes. After a moment, I realized I was flat on my back, looking up at the fly loft above the stage.

"She's coming to," Marie said.

I blinked and took in Jen, Marie, and Tyler hovering over me with concerned looks on their faces.

"Why did the music stop?" I asked.

"*Waltz* is over," Jen said.

"Over?" I asked, struggling to sit up. I turned my head and looked toward the lights. "Oh no."

Onstage, Qi led Hilary to bow in front of the *corps de ballet* line. Applause poured from the house.

"You fainted, and Hilary went on and finished for you," Tyler said from behind Jen and Marie.

My head was exploding.

"It's okay—" Marie started.

I interrupted her. "I have to get out of here."

"Let me help you," Jen said, following me as I stood and ran.

"Me too," Marie said, hobbling behind us. We hurried along the narrow passageway behind the backdrop.

I was still dizzy and nauseous. "This is so embarrassing," I said. When I tripped over a wire, Jen grabbed my arm to keep me from falling.

The dressing room was deserted. "Don't cry yet," Marie said.

I ripped off my costume and headpiece. Jen swept my makeup and hair supplies into a bag while I changed into my tracksuit.

"I can't believe this happened," I sobbed.

"We heard you were sick," Marie said, her voice full of sympathy. "Tyler was worried about you."

"Being sick is no excuse," I said, sliding my feet into my flip-flops and trying not to vomit. "And since when does Tyler care that much?"

"I think he cares a lot," Marie said. But I didn't want to think about him.

We started down the hallway and froze when we heard the clicking of Vivienne's shoes. She was coming, presumably to look for me.

The clicking grew louder. We exchanged glances.

"This way," Jen whispered, pushing open an emergency exit door. The alarm didn't sound. We left the theater as quickly as possible.

We ran right into my parents. They were standing outside the theater, looking worried.

"There you are," Dad said.

"What happened?" Mom asked, her voice full of concern. She turned to Jen. "One minute, she was dancing, and then halfway through the ballet, another girl ran on in her costume."

Jen explained that I fainted.

"It was very dramatic," Marie added.

While they introduced themselves, my mind wandered back to the moments before I fainted. If only I had pushed harder. If only I hadn't been so weak.

"I'll say goodbye now," Marie said. "Feel better."

I hugged her. "Thanks for your help," I said.

Jen apologized that she had to return to work and said, "I'll see you back in the room late tonight."

My parents walked me inside the dorms. "Did you see The *New York Times* review this morning?" Mom asked. "There's a picture and a nice mention of you."

"They called you 'piquant,'" Dad added.

"At least they didn't review today," I said. "They don't praise a dancer who passes out halfway through the show."

The hallways were deserted because everyone else was watching *Fire* at the theater. When we reached my room, I looked in the mirror. Tears and makeup ran down my cheeks. My French twist was falling apart. "I look as good as I feel," I said, unpinning my hair.

They watched me wipe my face with a wet washcloth. "You can go," I said. "I need to rest."

Mom insisted I shouldn't be alone, but Dad put his hand on her arm to say she should let it be.

I lay down on the bed. "Feel better," Dad said as they turned off the light. "We'll call you in a few hours." The door clicked closed behind them.

When I was alone, I cried my eyes out. There was no way I'd get in anywhere now.

I dreamed of Stacy Hannah dancing *Fire* until the phone woke me up. Every muscle in my body ached. The phone rang and rang and finally fell silent. I thought of all the years I planned to be a dancer and how all my hard work amounted to nothing.

And then the phone rang again.

I was still half-asleep but dragged myself out of bed to answer it. "Hello?"

"This is Madame Sivenko," said the voice on the line. My stomach knotted. "Come down to my office immediately."

I dreaded the thought. "I'm sick."

"This isn't a request," she said firmly. "Five minutes." The receiver clicked.

I walked over to the mirror, wondering how to proceed. For a moment, I stood there, staring at myself with terror rising in my chest. I decided I'd better brush my hair.

The whole day felt like a nightmare. I went to the elevator and rode down to the fifth floor, sure I was about to be expelled or worse. I was so scared I started to hyperventilate.

When I exited the elevator, the hall smelled like Simon's pipe, a sure sign that the teachers were in a conference.

There was a small crowd standing by the front desk. Nicole's mom was hugging an elderly woman. I guessed the crowd was Nicole's family because I saw Nicole in the center, tears streaming down her face.

"Ballet New York," Nicole's mom said to the other woman. "My daughter, your granddaughter, an apprentice with Ballet New York. I'm so proud." They celebrated with more hugs and tears.

Leave it to me to be miserable in the face of so much joy.

I hurried past their group, thinking Victor must have hired Hilary, too. She was a hero now, thanks to me, and her Mom was a significant donor. How could he not?

The foyer in front of Madame Sivenko's office was deserted. Inside, Madame Sivenko was behind her desk, fiddling with her diamond necklace and talking to Vivienne and Simon, whose backs faced the door.

". . . learned *Fire*—" Vivienne was saying.

"There you are," Madame Sivenko interrupted, seeing me in the doorway.

"I can wait outside," I said.

"No, come in," Madame Sivenko said, standing up as Vivienne swiveled in her chair and looked at me. Simon puffed away on his pipe.

I lingered outside her door. "I'm so sorry about the performance. I had a fever."

"We heard you were sick," Vivienne said, and her voice was surprisingly kind.

Madame Sivenko walked around the desk. "We'll leave you two alone."

Confused, I stepped forward into the office. At that moment, a man with silver hair stood up from a chair behind the doorway.

William Mason was not tall or cold like Victor Caldwell. He was in his sixties, with a strong jaw, intelligent eyes, and the most charismatic manner I'd ever seen. We'd never met, but I knew him instantly. I'd studied pictures of him since I was a little girl.

"Thanks, Natasha," William said. His voice was gentle but commanding, and I was drawn to him immediately. "We'll only be a few minutes."

The shock registered as Madame Sivenko, Simon, and Vivienne left the room. Vivienne squeezed my arm as she passed me.

"I enjoyed your performances this weekend," William said, offering me his hand. I thought of the rejection letter I'd received from Los Angeles Ballet Theater after the company audition. So why this strange meeting?

I apologized and said I was sick, declining to shake his hand.

"Could we sit for a minute?" He gestured to a chair, and we sat across from each other.

I had no idea why I was there or what I was supposed to say. The day grew crazier by the hour.

"Stacy Hannah is a big fan of yours," he said. There was a pause like he thought I'd say something, but I was too surprised to form a response. At last, he continued with a sentence I'll never forget as long as I live. He said, "I'd like to offer you an apprenticeship with my ballet company."

Somehow, I managed not to cry. Instead, I nodded and listened while he shared information I knew. He said that LABT had forty-five dancers, danced Roizman ballets and new works by resident choreographer Simone Reese, and in the fifteen years since its inception, had already become one of the top five companies in the United States.

"The contract is thirty-five weeks," he said, "We need you to start as soon as possible."

When I didn't say anything, he smiled with a glint in his eye.

"Here's my card," he said. "Please let me know in the next day or two if you'll be joining us."

"OK," I finally managed. "Thank you."

"You can also call our company manager if you have further questions. If you accept, we'll overnight your contract. You'll need to sign and return it by the end of the week."

He stood up, so I did, too.

His eyes studied me intently while I said I understood and thanked him. He smiled and replied, "I look forward to working with you."

With that, a whole new world opened for me.

Vivienne was waiting for me by the elevator when I came out of the meeting with William. "Congratulations," she said. "Did you accept?"

I told her I needed to think and discuss it with my parents.

"You should take the contract," she said. "William's a legend, and his company is doing remarkably well. This is a real job, what you wanted." She lifted my chin with her finger to make me look her in the eye.

"I know," I said. "I can't believe it."

She gave me a stern look. "Believe it."

"Can I ask you a question, even if it's ridiculous?" I asked, thinking of Jen and Jesse and how I'd watched them process the same issue.

She raised her eyebrow.

"Did I ever have a chance at BNY?"

"Take the job, Anna," she said. "Don't be a fool. Most of your classmates aren't getting one, and this is the top school in the country."

I was grateful and told her so. So many times, Vivienne helped me by saying to move forward and keep going. I'd always been able to count on her to tell me the truth.

My eyes met hers one last time before the elevator door shut. I could tell she was proud and happy for me, too.

CHAPTER 16

I went outside to call my parents at their hotel.

Mom answered with, "How are you feeling?"

"Still sick, but it's not important. I got a job. Mom, *I got a job*."

"Of course, it's important—wait. What are you talking about?"

That's when it sunk in that the news went way beyond me. "William Mason offered me a job with Los Angeles Ballet Theater." Just saying the words filled my heart with the promise of so much yet to come.

"You're kidding," Mom said, her voice turning giddy. "Really?"

"Fainting and all?" Dad asked in the background.

"Really," I said, as they shouted in celebration. "I made it."

Even with a fever, I felt like the luckiest girl in the world.

Because I was still sick, I took my dinner to go from the cafeteria. Tyler appeared as I was walking toward the elevator. A woman I assumed was his mother was with him. She had short blonde hair and a stern face that looked nothing like his.

"Is it true about Los Angeles?" he asked.

Word traveled fast. "It is," I said. "Congratulations on your contract, too." I hugged him and asked, "Will you introduce me to your mom?" I turned and offered her my hand.

"I've heard so much about you," she said in a kind voice, and I found her warmer than he'd described her. She clasped my hand between her own.

"Congratulations," Tyler said. "I'm so happy for you."

"I can't believe it."

"I can," he said softly. His mom put her arm around his shoulder, but he shrugged her off.

She looked hurt but turned to me and said, "It's exciting news."

We exchanged a smile. "Life is surprising these days."

"It sure is," Tyler said, staring at me, and we held each other's gaze for a long time.

The following day, I called the number on William's business card. His secretary said he was in rehearsal and instead put me on to George Summers, the company manager. I accepted the job offer and became a professional dancer at eighteen.

"I'm sure you're happy to have your friends Faye and Hilary joining you," George said at the end of the call. "See you in Los Angeles."

"Hilary?"

I was so dumbfounded that I hung up the phone without saying goodbye.

I'd never even been to Hilary's suite, not once in the entire year. Her single looked the same as our double had the year before, and the sight of her TV and her other familiar possessions brought back bad memories.

She was packing, and so was her mom, whom I'd never met. They had the same red hair and freckles.

Hilary was surprised to see me. I introduced myself to her mom, who said rudely, "You're the roommate from last year and the one who got sick," and returned to pulling Hilary's clothes out of the closet and folding them.

I turned to Hilary and said, "Thank you for finishing *Waltz* for me. Truly. I owe you."

Hilary was on the floor sorting pointe shoes and didn't respond, but she sat up straight when I followed with, "I just accepted a job in Los Angeles, and the company manager said you're going too."

Her confused expression almost made me laugh. She and her mom exchanged a look of consternation.

"Congratulations," I said, "Is there anything in particular you think I should know?" From the look on her face, I could see she was unhappy. Whether it was more about LABT instead of BNY, or me, I couldn't tell.

After a pause, she said, "Congratulations to you, too. I'm glad I could help with *Waltz,* and I hope you're feeling better. Did you know LABT is a non-union company that follows union regulations? We don't get to join the dancer's union like the BNY dancers."

"I heard," I said, leaning against her bed. "But we'll have a weekly salary, health insurance, and a retirement fund. Do you have your passport? We'll need it if we tour abroad."

"The upcoming season only has domestic tours on the schedule," she said.

"William said the company has plans to go to Europe in the next few years."

Hilary's mom interrupted, "Are you graduating YAH tomorrow?"

"Yes, I am."

"I already got my GED," Hilary said.

There was an awkward silence. "I'm so excited," I said finally. "I guess I'll see you in LA."

"Right," she said and returned to her shoes, giving me my exit cue.

Walking down the hall, I wondered what had happened with her and BNY. Sure, she'd bought her way into an extra performance, but as it turned out, she couldn't buy Victor.

The contract and season schedule came overnight. I signed on the dotted line, and on Wednesday morning, I FedExed the contract back to Los Angeles.

Dad flew home to Rock Island the morning after I graduated from YAH. "I'm sorry I can't go with you and Mom to LA," he said as Mom hailed him a cab. "Work calls." He hugged me, and then he was gone.

"I'm sorry I haven't been in touch," Rachel said when she answered the phone. "Life is so busy with graduation and this big tennis tournament. Did I tell you I'm going to Iowa? I got in. It's such a relief."

"That's great," I said. "I'm happy for you. My big news is I got a job. I'm heading to LA to join Los Angeles Ballet Theater."

"Your parents aren't making you go to college?" she asked.

I pictured her making the face I'd known for so long, that look that meant, "Why do you have to be so different?"

If I thought I didn't fit in with kids my age before, I certainly didn't fit in with them now.

"If I'm going to do this, now is the time," I said.

She said, "I feel like you're missing out on so much."

"I can't pass up this opportunity."

"I could never do what you're doing," she said.

"Honestly, Rach," I said, "I don't know how to do any-thing else."

Jen had convinced her parents she was in NBT for the long haul, so they bought her a condo as a graduation present. She moved her stuff out slowly. Her half of the room looked more and more bare.

I helped her carry bags of clothes up Columbus Avenue. We sat on the wood floor in her new, unfurnished studio and ate pizza, gossiping about movie stars and who was dating whom. It wasn't the time to talk about regrets and disappointments, not when so much lay ahead for both of us.

"Maybe you'll end up friends with Hilary in LA," she said, handing me a soda. We rolled our eyes and laughed.

"You better come and visit," I said. "Faye and I decided to be roommates, at least for the first year."

"I bet you'll get another chance to dance the lead in *Fire* after a few years," she said. "It's in their repertoire."

"Let's time it for when you get to dance *Giselle*."

I looked out the window at the city lights, already missing New York.

Jen walked me down the stairs of her brownstone. I thought of when I first met her on the plaza a year and a half earlier and how defeated I'd been then.

"We've come a long way," we said simultaneously when we reached the stoop.

"Why couldn't we have ended up in the same place?" she asked. But the truth was, it was better that way. We'd never have to compete.

"It's like we went through the army together," I said.

"We did, in a way," she said, and we hugged each other tight.

On my walk back to the dorm, I passed the fountain at Lincoln Center and dug a penny out of my purse. I closed my eyes. Taking a deep breath, I tossed the coin into the water.

When I leaned over to check where it went, there were hundreds of pennies at the bottom.

In the middle of my last night in New York, I lay awake, unable to sleep. The room was empty without Jen, and the lights from the city poured in through the window and illuminated the room. I kicked off my blankets. Even in my tank top and pajama shorts, I was sweating.

There was a knock on the door.

"Who is it?" I asked. "It's the middle of the night."

Tyler said, "Open up."

I climbed out of bed and let him in. He looked just as sweaty in pajama pants and a white T-shirt.

"I was hoping your air conditioner worked better than mine," he said.

"No such luck," I said. "I can't sleep at all. Didn't you, Jesse, and Qi move into a new apartment?"

"We don't get our key until tomorrow," he said. "Can I come in?"

He walked in and sat on the bed. I closed the door and sat facing him, crossing my legs. We looked at each other for a while and said nothing.

Finally, he said, "I can't believe you liked Jesse."

"I have no idea what you're talking about," I said, keeping a straight face.

"Of course you don't."

"Hold it," I said. "Are we friends again?"

He had the nicest smile. "We'll always be friends."

I lay down. "Let's get some sleep."

He waited, looking at me, and after a minute, he put his head on the pillow next to mine. I let my finger run down the inside of his arm. We took a deep breath.

After a while, I curled up into him, and we fell sound asleep, wrapped in each other's arms.

He was gone when I woke up, and I understood. It was too hard to say goodbye.

I showered and put the last of my things in my suitcase. My mom was in the lobby. "Today's a big day," she said.

I hailed a taxi and told the driver, "JFK airport, please."

We watched the skyscrapers fade as we left the city behind. The moment was bittersweet. I pictured myself in my lavender *Waltz* tutu, a million tiny rhinestones in my hair, bowing my head in a *grand révérance* to that essential chapter in my life.

I was grateful that graduation wasn't the end. I'd learned so much in New York, and after everything I'd been through, I was ready for the next step.

We were on our way to Los Angeles, and it was time for my career to begin.

About the Author

Miriam Landis is a faculty member at the Pacific Northwest Ballet. She was a LitCamp fellow and an assistant editor at Simon & Schuster, Hyperion, and the Amazon Books team. A Stanford grad, she was also a student at the School of American Ballet and a professional ballerina with

© Dan Lao

Miami City Ballet. When not writing, teaching, or dancing, she enjoys life on Lake Washington alongside her husband and four children. In addition to *Girl in Motion,* she is the author of *Girl on Pointe* (previously published as *Breaking Pointe*) and a middle-grade novel, *Lauren in the Limelight.* Learn more at www.miriamlandis.com.

I hope you enjoyed this book. Would you do me a favor?

Like all authors, I rely on community support
and online reviews to encourage future sales.
Your opinion is invaluable. Would you take a few
moments now to share your assessment of my book
on social media and the review site of your choice?
Your opinion will help the book marketplace
become more transparent and useful to all.

As ever,
Miriam